THE ELF [illegible]
FORGOT ABOUT
CHRISTMAS

the second novel from

Josh Baldwin

JOSH BALDWIN

UK | USA | CANADA | AUSTRALIA | BRAZIL | SPAIN | ITALY | GERMANY | FRANCE | JAPAN | INDIA | CHINA

joshbaldwin.org

10 9 8 7 6 5 4 3 2 1

First Edition

Books by Josh Baldwin

Becoming You And I

The Elf Who Forgot About Christmas

This book would not be the book it is today,

if it wasn't for my sweetheart, who not only helped shape it,

but helped to ensure I did it full-stop.

For cheering me on, hugging me at the end of long days,

for telling me the stress will be worth it, for making me smile,

I dedicate this book to you,

Daniel Kent.

I love you.

1

IT WAS A busy time of year in the North Pole. It was the First of December, which meant that it was an extremely stressful time for Father Christmas. He was stacked out with work to do and snowed under from all the organising he had to do. There were so many presents to make sure were all ready on time, that he felt as though he didn't know whether he was coming or going!

Dec 1st	*Dec 2nd*	*Dec 3rd*	*Dec 4th*	*Dec 5th*	*Dec 6th*	*Dec 7th*
Xmas Tree Goes Up		~~Mince Pie Tasting~~	Meeting with Head Elf	Mince Pie Tasting	Date Night at North Pole Square with Mrs. Clause	Igloo Repairs

Dec 8th	*Dec 9th* Wrapping Paper Re-stock	*Dec 10th*	*Dec 11th* Meeting with Head Elf – bloomin' elf busy!	*Dec 12th* Meeting with Head Elf	*Dec 13th* Ice Skating at Slippery Slopes	*Dec 14th*
Dec 15th Sleigh Maintenance	*Dec 16th*	*Dec 17th* Reindeer Haircut	*Dec 18th* Meeting with Head Elf – LAST ONE!	*Dec 19th* ELF CHRISTMAS DO!	*Dec 20th* Meal at The Red Nose	*Dec 21st*
Dec 22nd	*Dec 23rd* Reindeer Briefing	*Dec 24th* *CHRISTMAS EVE*	*Dec 25th* *CHRISTMAS DAY!!!*	*Dec 26th* …AND relax!	*Dec 27th*	*Dec 28th*
Dec 29th	*Dec 30th*	*Dec 31st* Last Day of Month – Pay Day				

Of course, in the North Pole it was also *very* cold and *very* snowy, but when December rolls around the snow thickens, the cold becomes more sharp, and the ice becomes dangerous.

The Elves, however, liked to think they were experts at being able to deal with these conditions. Santa, however, liked to call them fools, but he also knew it was none of his business – as long as the jobs that he wanted to be done, were done, then he was **more** than happy. The way in which they were done – well, *that* was up to the Elves.

Right now, on this First Day of December, they were putting up decorations around the North Pole. They had put reefs on every front door, lights around every window, tinsel around every lamp-post. They had put turkeys in the butcher's display, huge cakes in the bakers, and lit every candle at the candlestick makers. They had *even* remembered to put a star on top of every small Christmas tree that had been sprung up around the North Pole. The village had been decorated, they were ready for business, and for Christmas.

Except for **one** thing.

This thing – well, it was the most important thing of all!

This was the *North Pole Town Square Christmas Tree* – it was the spectacle of every year, the focus of the town, the tree that got *everybody* talking and *everyone* excited.

Every year there was the pressure to make the tree bigger than before, have it taller, thicker, with more lights and more tinsel and more baubles than ever before!

This year, the Head Elf, Mr. Frederick Jingelton himself, had cast a magic spell over the tree to grow it beyond what a tree could EVER *naturally* grow – the rumour that he would be doing this had spread around town since the very minute last year's Christmas tree had been taken down, and he had NOT wanted to disappoint.

Crowds had formed around the Town Square, and it had become so busy that Frederick had employed big strong Security Goblins with large barriers to come help secure the area. It was stressful enough as it was, putting the giant Christmas tree up, and that wasn't even including putting the decorations on, or even managing to get the star on top of it, without having hustle and bustle of hundreds and hundreds of Elves about.

His ElfSpeak - a small box that was clipped onto the top pocket of his green coat — made a squawking noise, and Frederick pressed a button down on the top.

"Mr Jingelton, Sir?" came a squeaky voice through the device.

Frederick pressed another button down and spoke. "Yes Goose?"

"Just to let you know your tree has arrived. We're going to get the Tucker to back up."

Frederick nodded, then he shook his head side to side, then pressed back down on the button, remembering Goose couldn't see him. "Sounds good to me, Goose."

Goose was a plump Elf who had worked his way up through the ranks, very quickly and was a very organised Elf indeed. He had been made Frederick Jingelton's Personal Assistant three Christmases' ago. It had become very clear to Santa Claus that Mr. Jingleton was taking a little bit of time settling into the job of being the newly-appointed and promoted Head Elf. Goose was secretly of opinion that if it wasn't for him, then Mr. Jingleton would have been fired from his job a long time ago, but Goose didn't like to make a fuss.

You see, the thing about Goose was that nobody really took him seriously. He was old, plump, with bright red cheeks and white hair sprouting out of his ears. He had a beard that looked as though it could have done with a bit of a trim, and he always wore the most disgusting coloured trousers that were so brightly coloured, many people thought they shouldn't be allowed— canary yellow, hot pink, vivid green, electric blue — but Goose was Goose and there was no changing him, no matter how much anybody were to try.

There was also the small matter that Goose, although maybe funny-looking by appearance, was a prime example of the saying that "you should never judge a book by its cover". Goose was a very intelligent Elf, and when it came to organisation — well, he could have organised the busiest, the most stressful and the most complex of any event with his eyes closed! Heck, he could probably do it in his sleep! So that was why nobody said anything to Goose, because they knew they needed him. They didn't want to upset him. He was as innocent as could be; he wouldn't hurt a fly!.

Goose was happy where he was — he could, quite easily, have Mr. Jingelton's job if he wanted it, but he didn't like the idea of all that responsibility. Being Mr. Jingelton's PA meant that he was free of having any of the blame put onto him if anything was to go wrong and that was just how he liked it.

Frederick stood back as the crowds began to part, and two long lines of goblins with their pointed chins and sharp noses came marching through. Goblins were frightening creatures if you got on the wrong side of them (that's why they made the best beings to be security), but respect them and listen to what they had to say, and you would have no issues at all. They had been the North Pole security for several generations now, and goblins as a rule lived for longer than anything else in the North Pole. People had grown up knowing to respect the goblins.

They all stood, although short but strong, shoulder to shoulder, and branched in both directions, until they were a distinct clearing that resembled a runway through the middle of the crowd.

"I think we're just about ready now, Sir," came Goose's voice down Frederick's ElfSpeak.

"Good good," replied Frederick. "Bring in the tree."

The crowd had fallen silent once they had all finished shuffling back and re-organising themselves after they had been moved by the goblins, and they all heard Mr. Jingelton give the order. An excited murmur rippled through the crowd, then everybody fell silent, their necks stretched and their heads craned back as they looked up to the sky expectantly.

Despite the fact they were many, extremely pretty and very lush Christmas trees that grew in and around the North Pole Village, the North Pole Town Square Christmas tree was highly valuable, and even more so now it had been enchanted to enhance its growth, and because of the fact it's never a normal Christmas tree that the Head Elf selects, it would make it so very obvious which tree it was that would be being used.

So, for that reason, the North Pole Town Square Christmas tree was selected and grown and tended to in a secret location — somewhere many miles away, and a place that changed every year so that nobody who shouldn't see it, should stumble across it, or harm it in any way. Mr. Jingelton, every year, in the run up to the First of December, would be laid awake in his bed, unable to sleep, stressing, tossing and turning over the thought that somebody would come along and chop off bits of the tree in the middle of the night — and, when he did eventually manage to fall asleep, he'd soon be woken up by nightmare after nightmare of somebody coming along with an axe, cutting down the tree, and stealing it. He could just imagine going along to collect the tree at the end of November, in preparation for the big day, only to discover nothing but a tree stump left and footprints in the snow left by the thief… a shudder went down his spine. It wasn't worth thinking about. It was too unbearable.

A sound buzzed through the night, and the crowd starting whispering and muttering excitedly, and then everybody started pointing.

In the night sky, a small white dot had appeared, and as everybody stood, waited and watched, the light continued to grow in size, getting bigger and bigger, until it was many lights, like a bright constellation of stars.

A moment or two later, and the lights were so bright that people were squinting and the roaring sound of engines filled the night sky.

"Bring her in, Tucker," Mr. Jingelton heard Goose say to the driver. "You're clear for landing."

At that, the Lorry-Sleigh began its descent, and everyone watched as a sleigh pulling behind it a huge flying trailer aimed at the space between the crowds got lower and lower, closer and closer, to the ground, until finally—

PLUMPF!

Snowflakes and frost were sent in all directions, the sleigh-lorry went hurtling down the makeshift runway, until it eventually came to a stop. It turned around and then slowly backed up to the Town Square podium, where the tree was going to go.

And the tree — well, the tree itself was marvellous, and HUGE.

Usually, everyone would be chattering and pointing and shouting about the tree — how good it was, how green it was, how big it was — but this year?

This year nobody was talking. Every Elf was in too much shock at the sight of it, the sheer size of it.

An entire family of a dozen elves could have built their cottages in its branches and lived a very happy life and none of the branches would have sagged from the weight. The trunk itself would take at least nearly a minute to walk around. The needles on it were the length of some of the goblins. It was the biggest, best, grandest, most impressive tree anybody had ever seen…

The silence lasted for one more minute as everyone took in the shock of this new sight, then they burst into applause!

They clapped and they cheered and they chanted Mr. Jingelton for a long, long time.

“Where did you manage to find that beast?” called one Elf.

“I didn’t even know trees could grow that big!” shouted another.

“How have you managed to keep it hidden for all this time?” yelled a third.

Mr. Jingelton just smirked to himself. It really was a spectacle, he had to admit, he was proud of himself.

The only thing now, though, was that he had to get the tree, well, up, which he had a feeling wasn’t going to be the easiest thing in the world to do.

“Let’s get her up, Goose.”

“Ready when you are, Sir.”

2

NOW THE THING about Elves is this: although they are very hard workers (nothing makes an elf more satisfied than getting a job well done) and their dedication to their work is never questionable, they always get far too over-excited.

Even Goose, who — as we know — is the most organised of all the Elves, had trouble containing his excitement over the Christmas tree. Nearly four times in a row the huge Christmas tree almost collapsed and fell to the ground, and who knew what type of damage it would have caused! If one of the branches had fallen off or splayed to the side it would have crushed half of the crowd or taken a roof off of one of the shops around the Town Square. If any of the needles had come away it could have empaled an elf or cut a goblin, and caused serious injury.

But none of the Elves seemed to think about this. Even Eric, the elf in charge of the Health and Safety Department, stood amazed next to Frederick, forgetting all the safety precautions he worked day and night to put into place. The plan they had come up with was that at several points from the bottom of the tree to the top they would tie ropes around it, then have a group of Elves pull on the ropes so that the Christmas tree was erected. They would then have several more Elves use magic to help lift the tree off the ground, as too much magic would be required from one small Elf due to the size of the tree, and then allow it to hover across the snow, into the centre of the Town Square, and plonk it down into a huge bucket, where it would be re-planted.

Putting it like that, it all sounded so simple, but that couldn't have been further from the truth.

"Not again!" yelled Frederick.

"Those Elves need to stop laughing and gazing at the tree, and start focusing on pulling the ropes," Goose said down his ElfSpeak. Frederick shook his head from side to side and buried his face in the palms of his hands as the tree was suddenly given a great big yank, and several needles came raining down into the crowd. Loud sounds of squealing came from the bustle, and a series of commotions occurred, but all the Elves found it highly amusing.

"Right," Frederick said, after watching the tree get SO close to be fully up, before it shook and nearly toppled over again, the elves who were pulling on the ropes almost being pulled into the air. "That's it. I've had enough. Eric — tell your team to control themselves or they'll be in big trouble."

The smile was suddenly wiped off Eric's face, and this time - instead of talking to the rope-pulling Elves through his ElfSpeak — he ran off, vanishing from sight to the other side of the tree.

"If word of this gets back to the big man," Frederick muttered to Goose, "it'll be more than just his coat that'll be red."

Goose nodded nervously, and then looked down at his clipboard.

They were running way off schedule, and there was nothing that he disliked more than going off schedule. Well, apart from parsnips and odd socks - he hated parsnips and odd socks.

"It's because of the size of the tree," Frederick continued. "If this is what they're like this year, I have no idea what they'll be like with next year's!"

Goose gulped at the sound of this. Surely there would become a point when the Christmas tree just couldn't get any bigger? If they continued on like this, they'd have to expand the size of the Town Square itself, and there would be no way Frederick would be able to handle a project on that scale. It would be a logistical nightmare. It didn't bear the thinking of. A shudder ran through his spine and he shook the thought from his head, returning back to the task in question.

In the end, Frederick and Goose got bored, and they decided that a little help from magic would do the trick. They got some goblins on hand to help pull more rope, and then secretly cast another spell on the tree and helped to push it up. The Elves on the ropes were beside themselves once the tree had been put into the bucket — they were convinced that they had been strong enough to do the job, and they had all come bounding over to Goose excitedly, giving out high-fives to the waiting crowds. Goose and Frederick glanced at each other, and decided it would be best to keep the truth to themselves and let the Elves think they had done it. After all, what harm could it do?

Now that the tree was in the bucket, the crowd simmered down, the Rope Elves settling. Everybody knew that this was it, the big moment... Nobody could misbehave now or get over-excited, at least not loudly.

"Everything looks safe and sound now," Eric said, walking back over to Frederick several minutes later. "The tree is secured."

Frederick nodded. "Thanks Eric." He patted him on the back. "We're ready, Goose."

Pressing down once more on the button on the top of his ElfSpeak, Goose bobbed his head in understanding and then spoke. "Janet — Janet, is that you? Oh, good. Yes, I'm fine thank you. Yes, of course it's cold, Janet. When is it not?"

Rolling his eyes, Frederick spun his hand in front of him to urge Goose on. "Anyway, Janet," Goose said, raising his voice slightly. "If you could let the boss know we're ready for him now, it would be greatly appreciated."

Janet's voice came down the ElfSpeak. "Certainly, certainly, Goose. Take care now. I've got a lovely knitted jumper to show you the next time I see you. I've buzzed Mr. C now. It's green and got robins—"

But what it was that the robins were doing on Janet's green, knitted jumper was anybody's guess, because Goose just closed his eyes impatiently, then turned the volume of his ElfSpeak down completely, so even if Janet was speaking, they couldn't hear her, and Janet didn't know.

Janet was Santa Claus' receptionist, and although she was lovely, she could talk all day long, and — if you let her — then she would.

Goose, admittedly, did like her, and he would often share a peppermint tea with her when they had their quarterly meetings four times a year to discuss Santa's, the Elves', and the Town's upcoming schedules and events, but right now time was of the essence and he didn't have time for jumper chats.

Right now, it was time for Mr. Claus to arrive.

3

IN THE MIDDLE of the crowd was an elf called Evergreen, who had pointy ears, blue eyes, rosy cheeks, and who was very cold. He could hardly feel his fingers, and twice he knelt down and prodded the tips of his boots, just to make sure that the tips of his toes hadn't fallen off. Despite being an elf, Evergreen did not feel equipped for this weather — he worked in the Paint Varnishing Department, which meant his job was to be in a nice, toasty room all day long, glossing over toys to make them look shiny and finished.

Santa'a arrival — much to Goose's horror —was even later than late, and he had a feeling that was due to Janet talking for longer than was needed, he bet, and that Mr. Claus didn't get the memo about the Town Square being ready as quickly as he should have done, or — at least — as promptly as Goose would have liked, but then Goose would have liked for the entire evening to have been done and wrapped up by this time, and there didn't seem to be a chance that was going to be happening anytime soon.

Evergreen was the latest Elf to have come of age and start working for Santa Claus and Co., and so this had been his first year working. He had enjoyed it so much, but this — this right now, stood waiting for Mr. C to give the big speech — was what he had been looking forward to the most. He had heard Santa give the speech before, but he'd not been able to be as close to the front as he was now. Employees were given the first priority of the front seats, with the other townsfolk being sent behind them. This meant that he was about to be as close to Santa Claus as he had ever been in his life, even though he had been working for him for the last twelve months. That was the thing with Mr. Claus; people often suspected that during the months of January to November he did nothing, but that could not be the furthest from the truth. He was extraordinarily busy all year round — although doing what, Evergreen had to admit to himself, he wasn't too sure, but he still knew that Mr. C was very busy.

When everybody started turning round, falling silent and stopping their whisper-filled conversations under their breaths, Evergreen spun on the spot, too, to see what everyone was looking at. He could feel his heart nearly burst through his chest as it begun to flutter and beat the fastest he had felt it do so since the day he first started working in the Paint Varnishing Department.

It was Mr. Santa Claus, the Father Christmas, himself.

He was dressed in his famous red suit, as always, and as he walked down the middle of the makeshift runway where the Christmas tree had come down, now that Tucker had moved the lorry, he nodded silently at the Elves, the Goblins, and the townsfolk as he went. He reached the stage that had been quickly put up by the rope-pulling Elves, and climbed up the steps. Evergreen could see that Santa looked immaculate — even from here, in the middle of the crowd, he could tell that Mr. C prided himself in keeping the upmost attention to his appearance. There was not a strand of white hair astray in his beard, a fleck of dust on his red coat, or a smudge or a smear on his shining black boots. His stomach was nice and round, and his hands were broad, and his cheeks were red, his eyes glittering and kind-looking, but even so, Evergreen knew he would be looking at everything, noticing anything. Nothing slipped away from the attention of Mr. Claus — Evergreen was sure that he must have eyes in the back of his head. He couldn't help but admire him. The man was a genius. He couldn't wait to hear him speak.

"Ladies and gentlemen," Santa started, and Evergreen grinned, his lips tugging up at the sides by an invisible force as though Father Christmas had cast an enchantment over them all. "It gives me great pleasure to be stood before you today, at the Annual North Pole Christmas Tree Ceremony. No matter how many years I do this, every year it continues to excite and delight me. This year, we have gone bigger and better than ever before, both in terms of the number of presents we are going to have to be delivering, and in the quality of the presents too. The same has been applied to the North Pole itself — this year, we have more lights up than ever before, more tinsel wrapped around our streets than ever before, and more baubles than ever before. Additionally, the same can also be said for our Christmas tree - the main focus of the village, and something we are extremely proud of.

"I am sure you are all astounded by the sheer size of it. For this, we have to thank our Head Elf, who — for another year — has managed to oversee our operations, and has helped make sure that everything, both in what you see and what you do not see behind the scenes, has been carried out smoothly with as few hiccups as ever."

At this, Evergreen noticed Mr. Jingelton shift from foot to foot rather awkwardly with a weak smile, and fiddle with his tie. He noticed him glance weirdly at his PA, Goose, and then look back out from the stage and over the audience. Evergreen always did think that there was something Mr. Jingelton was keeping to himself, but he never wanted to say anything. After all, he was a newly-appointed Elf working for Santa, and Mr. Jingelton and Goose had been doing this for numerous years — who was he to question anything? Evergreen shook his head, scratched behind his long, pointed ears, and turned his attention back to what Father Christmas had to say.

"How Mr. Frederick Jingelton has not only managed to find a tree as big as this one, but as to how he has successfully managed to get it here, where it will sit for the next month and amaze us all by its sight every day and night, is a logistical feat, and one that we must all appraise him for, and rightfully so, too."

The crowd started clapping and cheering for Mr. Jingelton, who just nodded and bowed slightly, looking rather stiff, Evergreen thought to himself. Next to him, Goose clapped happily, but his face seemed to paint a different picture. Evergreen pursed his lips in thought, but applauded anyway.

"And now, the penultimate part, we get to do my second-favourite bit of every year, and that's turning on the lights. As you know, every year somebody else who has never had this honour before is selected to illuminate the lights of the town and the tree, who we feel has worked extremely hard to ensure that Christmas is as special as it should be to the boys and girls all around the world. And so it gives me great pleasure to announce that Chester McBaubleton has been chosen by the Committee to represent the Elves in illuminating."

The crowd began to cheer once more, and there were a shuffle near the front of the audience as Chester McBaubleton began to awkwardly make his way through the crowd and toward the stage.

Evergreen and the rest watched as he slowly made his way up the stairs at the side of the stage and then walked across the platform, where he shook Goose's, Mr. Jingelton's, and Mr. C's hands, and then had a photograph taken with all that would be printed in the newspapers the next day, and then stood back, awaiting instructions.

He was given a button attached to a piece of cord that ran off the back of the stage and out of sight. Then, Santa clicked his fingers and, written in gold dust in sparkles in the air, a giant number '10' hovered in the sky.

"Ready, Mr. McBaubleton?" Mr. C asked.

Chester, who had knobbly knees and a runny nose, quivered and shook nervously, but nodded excitedly. He always did seem to be in a state of constant confusion and befuddlement, Evergreen thought to himself as he continued to watch, but he had really come on in leaps and bounds this year. For that reason, Evergreen supposed, it made sense to have let him be the ones who turned on the lights.

“Let the countdown commence!” Mr. C shouted over the crowds.

The huge golden ’10’ faded and was replaced by a ‘9’, then the glitters of gold shimmered and hurriedly turned into an ‘8’, shifted into a ‘7’, danced into a ‘6’, and so on and so on, accompanied by a chanting crowd, until it reached ‘0’, which exploded and burst out over the crowd as though a tonne of golden glitter had been fired out of the end of a cannon and began to rain and glimmer over them all.

Chester McBaubleton slammed the button, and the town hummed into life, bursting into light and life, every street-light illuminating, candles flickering, baubles glinting, Christmas lights shining, tinsel shimmering, shop windows brightened. The whole of North Pole Town came to life with brightness, and shone fiercely through the night, the snow seeming whiter and brighter, clearer and purer than ever before.

“Thank you ever so much, Mr. Baubleton,” Mr. C said, and Chester took a bow so low his pointed noise nearly touched the ground, and then he scrambled off the stage and vanished back into the crowd and out of sight once more. Around Evergreen, he could hear mutterings of people wondering how an Elf such as Chester McBaubleton had ever been chosen to do something as honourable as the turning on of the Christmas lights, and whilst Evergreen had to admit he agreed, there were a far more important part of the speech coming up that he was interested in — and he wasn’t the only one.

As Mr. Claus watched Chester McBaubleton leave the stage, he turned around to face Mr. Jingelton, who looked at Goose, who nodded at Mr. Jingelton, and who turned around in the opposite direction and nodded at Mr. C again, who then took a step forward back to the centre of the stage and began to speak. The crowd fell silent. You could have heard a pin drop from the front of the crowd if somebody had dropped one at the back.

"And now," grinned Mr. C, "for the bit that we all love. The part we all look forward to. The finishing touch, the creme de la creme of the decorations, the big one. It's the one we've all been waiting for — it's… the Christmas Star!"

Behind him, a huge trolley was rolled onto the stage, a flowing purple velvet cover hiding something that looked pointy and had five sharp parts sticking out of it in each direction. The two Elves pulled the trolley until it reached the centre of the stage, then they secured the trolley into place so it couldn't go anywhere. They locked the wheels, gave it a wiggle to test it, and then walked off, nodding at Santa as they did so. He bowed his head in thanks, walked around the trolley and back to the podium, where he resumed talking into the microphone.

Everybody was silent, everybody was waiting. If the Christmas tree was an important part of the Annual Ceremony, then the Star was even more important in comparison. This signalled the start of Christmas, and the beginning of the true hard work that everybody needed to put in.

"Now, as we know," Santa started to speak, recapturing everyone's attention again, "the star is very important. I wouldn't even like to tell you the price that this year's star has cost.

"Also, as you all know, every year myself and the Committee,

Mr. Jingelton here, as well as Goose, likes to select somebody who we think has worked hard, who has represented the Elf community, and has showed his or her full commitment to the year's work. This year, as we are all fully well aware, has been the busiest year so far — the world's population is expanding, with more children being raised than ever before. Standards are growing, skyscrapers erupting out of the ground, more money being made and printed than ever before. The machines and the factories are churning out toys, smoke billowing into the skies. Targets are being set and huge business-people are pumping money by the billions into Christmas. The festive season is getting tougher and tougher every year, and whilst we may all be in the same bubble here, working as hard as ever before, the world out there is ever-changing, ever-growing, and ever-developing, and with demand going up we have to work harder than ever before too, to continue making a difference, to deliver on time, and make those children smile, to make sure they have the Christmas that they remember — to make sure they have the Christmas they deserve. Because that's the real reason we do all this — forget about the targets, forget about the demands, forget about the competition — and just think of that one child. That one child that we picture in our minds when we do this, and the smile on that child's face when they open their Christmas present on that Christmas Day morning, pulling back the paper and slipping off the ribbon, their faces becoming illuminated and full of life because of the joy that they find within it. That — that — is the reason why we do what we do."

"Therefore, my team and I choose an Elf every year to be the one

— the only one — to put the Star on top of the tree. It is the sign of the most ultimate respect, and the symbol of the upmost recognition. Mr. Jingelton, when you're ready."

Everybody stood with baited breath, watching and waiting, taking in Santa's speech and feeling pride swell inside of them as they thought about what he had said, about what they did, and about that one child. Elves did not work for money, they did not work to buy cars, they did not work to serve themselves — happiness was the currency they ran on, and if they could make people happy, then that was all they wanted, all they needed, and everything else they needed to have a happy life — well, that was what Mr. Claus and the North Pole Village provided for them. As long as the children of the world were happy, then so were the Elves of the North Pole, too.

Goose pulled an envelope out of his coat pocket, and handed it to Mr. Jingelton, who walked across the stage to Santa, the sound of his boots clipping against the wooden stage being the only sound. He passed Santa the envelope, and then walked back, resuming his position next to Goose.

Brightly golden, the envelope was small and neat. Santa looked down at it, then glanced back up at the audience of Elves looking expectantly up at him. He raised the envelope up ahead of him, and slipped it open.

Evergreen and the others watched as he pulled out a small slip of card, then cleared his voice, and then spoke into the microphone.

"It gives me the upmost pleasure to announce that this year's Elf of the Year, our Star Elf in both senses of the word, is Evergreen Frostly!"

The whole world slowed down, and the crowd burst into applause, and Evergreen found himself in a state of confusion, not being able to believe what it was that he had just heard.

Could it be true?

Was this real?

Had he really been made the Elf of the Year?

He didn't believe it.

He wouldn't believe it.

4

BEFORE EVERGREEN KNEW what was happening, everybody was clapping, turning around and looking at him, he had no choice but to move. He had to walk to the stage — then it all suddenly dawned on him what this really meant. He would have to be the one to put the Star on the top of the tree — but how would he do that? Especially with all these people looking at him, with the tree being so big, the star being so special, and all this pressure and responsibility put on him. His knees began to quiver and knock against one another, and he was sure he would not, could not, be able to do this.

Evergreen willed himself to walk. As he began to move, his legs finally behaved his feet going one step in front of the other. The crowds, all still cheering although for some reason Evergreen couldn't hear anything, as though he had been submerged underwater with everything moving slowly and sounding fuzzy, parted way and split into two without even the help from the Goblins, and made a pathway for him to get to the stairs of the stage.

People nodded at him, cheered his name, patted his shoulders, whacked him on the back. They took photos of him, tugged at his clothes, playfully pushed him about, and made a great big fuss. He had only been working for Santa for a year, he thought to himself — there must have been a mistake made somewhere along the way. This surely couldn't be right — how could he have been chosen as the most committed, the most dedicated Elf? He was just Evergreen. Just little old Evergreen who was making his way through life, plodding along, and just trying his best. His work wasn't worthy of this. What about Cormack, the grumpy old elf from the Postal Department, who had worked there for the last fifteen years without so much as a promotion and had been labelling presents and stamping them for years? Or Brenda, from the Ribbon and Wrapping Design Department, who had designed more different types of wrapping papers and shades of colours for ribbons over the decades than you had probably changed your underwear! And then there was Derek, the elf who worked in the Naughty Or Nice Court Department, who dealt with making pleas for both children whose parents' had thought they had been wrongly judged and put on the Naughty List instead of the Nice List. This meant they had been sent a lump of coal and an orange if they were lucky, rather than their presents. He had even looked after Elves who had had a problem or an injury in the workplace and wanted changes to be made or compensation sent to their cottage. He had dealt with all sorts of surprising cases over the years — some of them shocking! — and yet not once — not once! — had he ever, ever, ever been given the chance to take the Star up to the top of the Tree.

All of this ran through Evergreen's head, distracting him and making him lose focus on what he was doing, so much so that before he knew it the silence was back, except this time the silence was real and not at all in his head, everybody had fallen quiet and was looking at him, waiting and watching.

He had reached the bottom of the stairs of the stage, somehow already, and now it was time for the moment of truth, the moment he had been dreaming about all of his life, ever since he had been just an young Elf and had watched his Dad in the crowd ahead, to see if he would be selected as Elf of the Year, the Star Elf, but not once had it ever happened — he was pretty sure that it hadn't happened to anybody in his family since dozens of generations ago, almost three centuries before now! — And yet now it was the moment he was dreading.

Looking up the stairs, the climb seemed huge. How was he going to climb up those steps without falling over, without stumbling, without making himself look silly? There were so many Elves that Santa surely could not remember all of them individually — although rumour had it that he could and did — and this might be Evergreen's only moment of talking to the big Mr. C in real life itself — he didn't want Santa to remember him for all the wrong reasons.

Taking a deep gulp of cold air, he raised his leg and began to climb. As he reached the top step, he looked out over the crowd and stepped onto the stage, and it hit him just how many people came to this event. For as far as his eyes could see, there were rows upon rows of Elves staring back at him, their eyes glazed over, following him as he made his way across the stage, the reflection of the dozens of twinkling Christmas lights that were illuminated around the Town Square reflecting back at him. He swallowed a little too hard and it seemed to be the loudest sound he had ever heard or made in his life, and then — BUMP.

He walked right into the podium that had the microphone attached to it that Santa was speaking into. He felt his cheeks erupt into flames. He had never felt so silly in his life. How would people forgot that now? He'd forever be remembered as the Elf who couldn't see where he was going, or the Elf that was too distracted by Christmas lights, or something else that was far too silly and far too not true. Kind of.

Fumbling with his hands, Evergreen cleared his throat and then took a step back, where Santa Claus himself — Santa Claus himself! The top man! The Big Mr. C — looked down at him, and smiled the biggest, kindest, smile you had ever seen a person smile. As Evergreen looked into his face, past his white beard, and his rosy cheeks, he noticed had the most warming eyes a person could ever have. They glinted with kindness and Evergreen could just tell that everything he had ever hear about Father Christmas was true — he cared about the Elves, he cared about Christmas, and he cared about the children and making them happy.

"Please welcome to the stage… Evergreen McFrostly!" Santa called out, then clapped his hands on Evergreen's back and turned them so they were both stood, looking out to the crowd.

They stood there for a moment, and then they burst into commotion, applauding and cheering. A storm of lights erupted into life at the bottom of the stage where dozens upon dozens of Elves with cameras took photograph after photograph. He could imagine his startled face on the front of the newspaper clipping he just knew his Mum would cut out and put in a photo-frame, and hang on the wall of her home for everyone to see for a very long time. The thought of it quickly made him smile.

"We have recognised the tremendous amount of work that Mr. E. Frostly — "

"Oh, please call me Evergreen, Sir," Evergreen said.

Santa smiled. "We have recognised the tremendous amount of work that young Evergreen here has put in during his first year of employment with us here in the North Pole. From the very minute on the first day he started, young Evergreen has had a key eye for detail and a keen drive to work. His standards have constantly been high, and not once has his productivity or his quality decreased. We are so very proud of you, Evergreen, and at such a young age too — in fact," and at this Santa stopped and turned around to look at the watching crowd, "young Evergreen here is our youngest Elf of the Year to have been selected by the Committee. Not once have we had an Elf as young as this, be the Star Elf. It is our greatest pleasure, Mr. Frostly, to present you with this certificate," He handed Evergreen a scroll, "and this trophy," He passed Evergreen a trophy that was red, green, gold and silver, and nearly weighed poor Evergreen down to the ground; it had the names of every Elf that had ever been awarded the Elf of the Year engrained upon it, "and the honour placing the Star…on the top of the tree."

Santa then took the scroll and the trophy away from Evergreen again, and passed them over to Goose, who passed them over to Mr. Jingelton, who passed them onto someone else, until they were hidden from view once more.

The trolley with the Star on was moved closer, and Santa finished his speech and then threw his hands up into the air, so that everybody followed his hands and looked up into the sky, and up, up, up to the top of the tree.

Evergreen gulped.

If the half a dozen steps had made him nervous on his entrance to the stage, then he would much rather do that a hundred times over, even if he knew he would fall up them or down them at some point, because those steps were nothing to what he was going to have to do now.

Next to the Christmas tree was the tallest ladder you had ever seen, to match the height of the tallest Christmas tree you had ever seen. It must have had at least four hundred steps on it, if not five hundred at least! And now that he was stood at the bottom of the Christmas tree, the top of it wasn't even visible. It made Evergreen feel funny as he tipped his head back to try and look at the top of it. It was so high it made him feel dizzy and he could swear he could feel the Earth actually spinning around and around and hurtling through space. The tree itself kept looking as though it was falling down to the ground, but that was just because of the thin wisps of clouds that were starting to drift over the Town Square and the Village. Evergreen shook his head and blinked his eyes and then looked at Santa.

"You mean…" he mumbled. "You mean I go up there?"

He had asked Santa the question in a tone of voice that Evergreen thought would show Santa that going up that ladder was the last place he wanted to be, but Mr. C seemed to have taken it to mean the complete opposite!

"That's right, Evergreen! It's our pleasure. Now, of course, the Star is too heavy for one person to carry on the ground, let alone whilst carrying it and taking it up a ladder. So, the Star will be hoisted up to the top for you to meet when you yourself get to the top, and then you'll be able to lean across, grab the Star, pull it down, and place it over the tip of the tree. Does that all make sense to you?"

…Meet the star at the top? Lean across and get it? Pull it down? Did Santa not know how heavy that Star was, how high the tree was, how dangerous it would be to lean across at that height?

"Evergreen?" Santa prompted, interrupting Evergreen's thought. "Are you ready?"

Evidently, Santa didn't seem to realise anything.

Evergreen just nodded.

What was he committing himself to?

5

MR. GRIT DID not like Christmas.

For as long as he could remember, Christmas had always been a cold affair, in both senses of the word. He did not like how cold it was, or how the ice made him slip over and fall on his bottom and look like a fool. He did not like it when he had been a young boy, when he had still been at school, and all the normal lessons and reading and writing stopped, just because Christmas was around the corner. He did not see the point of stopping learning just because a day where you gave out presents was going to happen. It was valuable learning time, he used to say to anybody that listened. Wasn't Christmas a waste of time, he used to ask? Wasn't Christmas just one big stress about money, he used to exclaim?

But nobody ever seemed to agree with him. They all just seemed to agree with one another and call him "Scrooge!"

"Haven't you ever heard of Charles Dickens?" one gentleman once said to Mr. Grit when he had been just a young boy and had earned a small income by polishing the boots of businessmen, who would sit there and moan and grumble and argue with him about Christmas with their faces covered up and hidden behind their opened newspapers.

"I have," nodded the boy.

"And do you know what the most famous story of his to have ever been written is?" the man asked.

The boy shook his head from side to side.

"A Christmas Carol," the man replied.

"A Christmas Carol?"

"A Christmas Carol! That's what I said, wasn't it, boy? You must have heard of it — with the three ghosts: the ghost of Christmas past, the ghost of Christmas present, and the ghost of Christmas yet to come?"

The young boy who was yet to grow into Mr. Grit suddenly realised what he had been talking about. "Yes, Sir. I have, Sir."

"Good," said the man, nodding triumphantly. "Well, he didn't like Christmas either, because he wanted to carry on working and to carry on earning money and he didn't like giving gifts either. And look where he ended up." As he said this, he nodded again, as though he had proven some sort of a point to the young boy who was polishing his boots.

The young Mr. Grit frowned and titled his head. "I'm sorry, Sir," he said, "but I'm not sure what your point is?"

"The point is," the man said, leaning forward in his chair and putting his newspaper down, "is that no good came to anybody who hated on Christmas and tried to bring down other people's merriment. It didn't get Ebenezer Scrooge very far, and if you carry on with the way that you are, it won't get you very far either. You'll just turn into the real life version of Mr. Ebenezer Scrooge, and I wouldn't like for that to happen to you. Heck, I wouldn't wish it on my worst enemy to turn out like him." The businessman shuddered as he spoke, and then returned back to his newspaper, pulling it slightly closer to his face than what was necessary and closer than it'd been before, which seemed to quite clearly show that, for as far as he was concerned, the conversation was finished with.

Shaking his head, the young Mr. Grit felt strange and not all himself after what the man had said to him, and as he carried on finishing polishing the businessman's boots, the conversation went round and round his head repeatedly.

However, the next day came and went on, and so did Christmas, and the year following, and that Christmas, and the Christmas after that, and the Christmas that, and so on and so on, and the conversation he had with the businessman was very quickly forgotten about.

With every Christmas that passed, Mr. Grit grew to dislike it more and more. He just could not understand it. His parents had never taken part in it, and their parents had never taken part in it either. If anything, Christmas was just the time of year when he was reminded of this fact, when he had to see everybody else take part and find it fun and festive, packed with cheerfulness, but there were no cheerfulness in December for Mr. Grit.

This continued on until Mr. Grit grew into adulthood, and then decided that he was going to be a full-time villain instead. For the last few years, he had been thinking of ways as to how he could bring down

Christmas, how he could stamp it out and make it stop. That was the plan.

He would do something that meant nobody got presents and he knew for the first few years there'd be uproar and anger and confusion, but time is a great healer, Mr. Grit often said, although for himself this couldn't be further from the truth, but he couldn't see that, and he thought that people would very quickly forget all about it, and go on with their lives, Christmasless. And a Christmasless life was just what he was after.

But for this to happen, he had to take one person down — one person who, year after year after year, continued to grow Christmas, to make it special, to deliver presents, forever reliable and trustworthy and oh so very, very cheery.

And that person — well, that person was Father Christmas.

Mr. Grit did not like Father Christmas. If it hadn't had been for Father Christmas, then Christmas wouldn't exist and Mr. Grit would not be in the predicament in his life that he had found himself to be in at this very moment. For Christmas to stop, he would have to go right to the top, and take down Father Christmas himself — Christmas couldn't be Christmas without Mr. Christmas, after all.

So, this year, Mr. Grit had laid out a plan, and then he and Crook, his assistant, had gotten the first flight to the North Pole. Crook was a goblin who had turned sour, who had once worked in the North Pole many, many years ago, but had been caught trying to steal some of the presents from under the noses of the Elves, who had quickly caught on and had told Mr. Christmas what was going on. Crook, who back then had been called Bing, couldn't believe that the Elves had snitched on him. It then all came out that it hadn't been the Elves who had told Mr. Christmas what had been going on, but rather an Elf called Bong.

Bong was Bing's twin elf brother, and Bing and Bong had been best friends when they had been child Goblins, but as they grew older and started to work, Bong loved working in the North Pole and producing presents and working for Father Christmas, but for Bing — well, Bing just didn't like it. He hated the fact that he had never been given the chance to be able to choose what it was that he wanted to do for the rest of his life. It was as though from the moment he had been born his whole life had been planned and mapped out for him, and the entirety of it from start to finish would take place in the North Pole and he would never leave, he was sure that there was more to life than that.

But Bong thought that this was wrong, and he meanwhile loved the Elves and the North Pole and working for Father Christmas, but Bing disagreed, said that the Elves thought they were better than the Goblins, and that he had had enough. The only problem was, no one had ever left the North Pole before - no one had ever wanted to - except for those who had been Banished.

That was why Bing had stolen from the Elves. He had to go the Department of Naughty or Nice, and the Court ruled that he had been Naughty. The crime was seen as bad, and he was Banished.

On his Banishment Day, Bong had stood and wept as Bing had packed his bags and left the North Pole behind him, venturing out into the snow to start a new life, and Bing had found what was supposed to be — to many — the worst day of his life, to be the best day of his life. He was free to go wherever he wanted and do whatever he wanted. He had come up with a brand new identity, changed his name to Crook from Bing, and then he was gone, and he had never been happier.

Upon coming to the big city, he had bumped into Mr. Grit. They both shared a common interest in disliking Christmas, and that had been that and they had hit it off from there. Mr. Grit had told Crook about his plan to bring down Father Christmas and the North Pole and to end the festive season for once and for all, and Crook had never heard a plan that sounded better. They had signed a deal and joined forces, and the rest is history, and now they were here, in this moment of time, and heading back to the North Pole — a place that Crook had never thought he'd return to.

It was much colder here than it had been back in the city. Crook had almost forgotten just how cold it could be in the North Pole, and as the iciness began to settle in and nip at his skin and bite at his nose and settle into his bones, all the memories of his time here came flooding back to him. Strange, it was, to think that this is where he used to live for so long.

Mr. Grit and Crook reached the top of a hill, and then below them a sight unveiled itself. It was the North Pole, and even Mr. Grit, who disliked Christmas and everything else to do with it, could not believe his eyes. This was the first time in his life he'd ever seen the North Pole with his own eyes.

For starters, it was bigger than he had ever imagined it to be, and so much brighter too. It seemed to be a huge ball of light, illuminating up in the darkness. The stars above it seemed to be shining brighter than anywhere else Mr. Grit had ever seen, and the snow appeared to be whiter and more pure. Hundreds of roofs of cottages and small homes could be seen, all of them a different shape and size and sloping off in a different direction to one another. It all looked like the front of a Christmas card. A church could be seen, calling out into the night, the ring of its bell echoing softly off the soft snow that ran off for miles and miles in every direction from the small village. Just behind it huge buildings could be seen, looking like parts of a castle, and Mr. Grit guessed that those were where Father Christmas and his Elves produced all of the presents that were sent out every year.

Then, in the middle of the Town, Mr. Grit squinted his eyes and saw the tip of a Christmas tree — and it must have been a huge Christmas tree, because even from here, where Mr. Grit and Crook were stood — the top of it seemed to tower over nearly all of the buildings that surrounded it. They were lots of lights shining on it and Mr. Grit could see hundreds upon hundreds of people stood all the way around it, spilling out of the Town Square and into every direction.

"We were right," Crook said, with a wicked grin. "The Star Ceremony — it's tonight."

Mr. Grit cackled. "Let's go cause some mischief, and say goodbye to Christmas as you knew it before."

Grit joined in with the cackling, and then the pair of them

vanished over the hill, and made their way to the North Pole Village, where everybody was stood happily without so much of an inkling as to what was about to happen next. Mr. Grit couldn't wait.

6

EVERGREEN WAS STOOD at the bottom of the ladder, and was looking up at it towards the top. It seemed to stretch on for an awfully long time, and he really wasn't very sure he was going to be able to do it. He could almost feel the eyes from the hundreds of people who were stood in the crowd boring into his back, and he felt an immense amount of pressure to do this.

After all, he had reminded himself, this is what he had been dreaming of for years. This is what the older Elves in his family would have loved to have been able to do. He knew there would be many, many more Elves in the crowd who were wishing they could be where he was right now, doing what he was about to do.

He took a deep breath, raised his leg, and climbed up onto the first step of the ladder. The audience erupted into applause. A small smile spread across his face.

"I can do this," Evergreen told himself. "I can do this, I will do this."

Music began to play from the band, The Candy Canes, that Santa had introduced to the stage just after he had brought Evergreen over to the ladder, and the crowd began getting into the Christmas spirit. Evergreen took a gulp of cool air, put his foot up above the other, then pulled his other leg up over it, and so on and so on, slowly making his way up the ladder.

He wasn't alone. Next to him the huge star was being hoisted up through the air, only moving up by a few inches at a time in synchronisation with Evergreen, so that he and the star would reach the top at the same time. He suddenly felt a tremendous amount of pressure to hurry up — he felt as though he was keeping a lot of people waiting.

When he reached what he thought was the halfway mark, the music that The Candy Canes were playing seemed to get louder and faster, and when he looked down the crowd seemed to be getting merrier and merrier. By now, he thought, they would have started to serve out the drinks — Elves loved drinks that were packed full of sugar, and as soon as they started drinking it they always tended to get a little bit silly, but continued drinking more and more of it anyway.

By the time he reached about a quarter of the way from the top, Evergreen stopped to catch his breath, and then took another look down at the ground. It seemed to spin underneath him, and he gripped the edges of the ladder harder than he had ever gripped anything before, turning his knuckles a bright white. He had known that the tree was tall from when he had been down below and looking up, but now that he was nearly at the top, he hadn't realised just how tall it actually was.

Feeling slightly sick from the height, his knees burning from all the steps, and his hands cramping because of the cold and from how tightly he was holding onto the ladder, he continued on until he was a few metres away from the very top of the ladder. He took another look down below, and half of him was glad to see that by now the crowds were mostly partying, dancing, singing and messing around, but the other half of him was kind of sad that nobody seemed to be paying him much attention. He hoped that they would do by the time he reached the top — he knew that this was supposed to be a big moment for him, but he didn't want to feel as though it had been wasted and missed by everybody. Evergreen himself had always loved watching the Star Elf of the Year put the Star on the top of the Town Square Christmas tree, but then he also supposed he had been too young in all the other years before now to be able to join them all in drinking the sugar drinks — you had to be a fully-grown Elf to be allowed to do that. The thought of it made him feel a little bit sulky — the very first Christmas that he could have drunk a sugar drink and got merry with all the others, and yet here he was, stuck up a ladder, in the freezing cold, unable to talk to anyone else, and all to put a star on the top of the tree - if Santa wanted a star on the top of his tree, then why couldn't he climb up here and put the star on the blasted tree himself...

He suddenly grew red in the face, and reminded himself of just who it was that he was thinking about in such an angry way. If it wasn't for Father Christmas then he wouldn't have been living the life that he was today, not only that, it really was such an honourable thing to be able to be called the Star Elf of the Year.

Swelling his chest up with newly-found pride and courage, Evergreen took one more last gulp of fresh air, and then sped up the remaining few rungs of the ladder, until he reached the top.

Next to him, the star, too, reached its maximum height, and then it must have rung some sort of an alarm down below, because suddenly Evergreen heard The Candy Canes stop playing their music, and a large spotlight appeared on him.

"Evergreen!" came a voice, and when Evergreen dared to look down below, he could see a red speck holding something small and black, that he guessed must be Father Christmas holding a megaphone. "Congratulations on reaching the top of the tree!"

Evergreen stuck his hand out and gave them all a thumbs-up, but then a surprise shock of wind came out of nowhere and took him by surprise, and he quickly drew his hand back in and took hold of the ladder again. "Whoa," he said aloud to himself.

"Now," Father Christmas continued, "when you're ready you need to lean forward, grab the two points of the star that stick out near the bottom, and then pull it into you nice and close. Then, when you've done that, you need to pull it down so that the tip of the tree slides into the bottom of the star, and pull it down and tightly so that the star is secure. If it falls off, it'll cause some damage from that height, and I don't want it to get broken for the price that it cost..." he added, mumbling to himself. "Or for an Elf to be hurt," he quickly added. Evergreen had a sneaky suspicion that someone such as Mr. Jingelton had reminded him to say that. (In reality, it had been Goose who had reminded Mr. Jingelton to tell Father Christmas to say that.) "So," concluded Father Christmas, "feel free to start when you're ready!"

Evergreen still didn't feel as though it was a good idea to lean across from being so high up on the tree. He then noticed on the bottom of the star was a small, black circle — he frowned at it and moved closer towards it, when he noticed it was a camera. A small light above it suddenly lit up red, and the realisation of what it was suddenly hit him.

He looked down, and he saw a huge televised version of himself looking down as well on a big screen that had been erected next to the stage, so that everybody could get a closer look and a better view of what he was doing and how he was doing it. No pressure then, he thought to himself.

Psyching himself up, he clenched his jaws and then exhaled, and then took one hand off the ladder. The wind all of a sudden felt so much stronger than before.

Then, slowly, he slipped his second hand off the ladder edge, and then teetered on the steps, swaying back and forth, back and forth, as he tried to regain his balance.

That was it, he thought to himself, as he dared to move himself closer to the star. He had done it. He had actually done it!

Evergreen then placed two hands on either side of the star, the huge television screen below broadcasting his smile out to the watching crowd and those small few in the North Pole who had chosen not to venture out of their cottages, or had decided to return to the comforts of their own homes once the sugar drinks had come out, and then he began to tug the star closer to him.

He looked down, and he momentarily felt dizzy again, but then he shook his head side to side and told himself to stop being silly.

“I can do this,” he muttered to himself under his breath so the camera wouldn’t hear him. “I can do this, I can do this, I can do this.”

The star was heavier than he had thought it would be, and he could feel his small muscles straining as he tried to pull it closer. The wind began to pick up again, and he could feel the tree start to sway side to side, back and forth, not by much but it was enough to put him off.

From down below he could hear the silence of the crowd began to fade, as slowly the watching Elves began to return to their sugar drinks and their conversations again, growing less interested in waiting to see Evergreen pull the star down.

He regained his energy and then pulled the star sharply. It jutted forward, and a gust of wind threatened to pull both the star and him away. He quickly let go of the star with one of his hands and grabbed hold of the ladder again, his feet cramping up from trying to stay gripping onto the ladder through his shoes.

“Steady, Evergreen!” called Father Christmas, shouting up through his megaphone.

Evergreen clenched his teeth and tried to stay calm. “I’m trying to be as steady as I can,” Evergreen replied, perhaps a bit more snappily than he had intended it to be.

Down below, Goose and Frederick glanced at each other and raised their eyebrows. Father Christmas’ eyes just widened, but he didn’t say anything else after that, much to the relief of Evergreen.

Evergreen then slowly retracted his hand back from the ladder and took a firm grasp of the two bottom points of the star. With a huge gulp of breath and a determined face, Evergreen pulled the star as hard as he could, closer, closer, closer, to him, and then down, down, down, and then —

He'd done it! The star was on!

The star was in position!

The spotlight was joined by two more spotlights that ran circles around Evergreen in congratulations, and Father Christmas began to speak as the audience erupted into applause once more and The Candy Canes started to perform again, even louder and with more energy than they were doing so before, but what was all happening Evergreen did not know.

The weirdest feeling that he had ever felt in his life washed over him, and then before he knew it everything was fading, and then he let go of the ladder —

And down he fell —

Down

Down

Down

Down he went.

Before he reached the ground, his world turned black…

7

MR. GRIT AND Crook made their way through the snow-drifts, iciness consuming the bottoms of their legs. Mr. Grit had not dressed for the situation, and he was — secretly — beginning to regret wearing his business suit. The hems of his trousers were getting wet and awfully cold. He was tall and thin, looking like the type of manic villain you would expect to see in some sort of a comic-book. He wore all black, except for his white shirt beneath his black blazer, and the small, folded-up white handkerchief in his blazer pocket on his breast. He prided himself on having a very neat villainous attire.

Crook, meanwhile, was small and stumpy. His legs were extremely short, and he found it very difficult to keep up with Mr. Grit, who, despite the snow and the cold and the wetness, was able to make great, long strides through the snow. He wobbled and stumbled and he was breathing heavily, struggling to catch enough oxygen, whilst trying to bobble along after Mr. Grit.

"Do you have to breathe so hard?" complained Mr. Grit.

"I can't help it," grumbled Crook.

"Not my problem," remarked Mr. Grit.

"What can I do about it?"

"That's for you to figure out."

Crook, although looking up to his boss and carrying a huge amount of admiration for him, rolled his eyes at Mr. Grit and then clamped his hand over his mouth in an attempt to keep himself quiet.

By the time they reached the edge of a ridge, Crook found himself feeling as though he was about to burst at any moment from holding his breath for so long, and he was happier than he had ever thought he would be at the sight of the North Pole Village. He released his hand from his mouth and a loud exhale came from him. Mr. Grit shot him a glance, but the sight of the village below stopped him from saying anything.

They were on top of a ridge, closer to the Village than they had been so before. It allowed them a perfect view of the Town Square below, with the Christmas tree and the ongoing Ceremony, but with the lip of the ridge in front of them it would make it very difficult for anybody below in the Town Square to be able to spot them, especially against the darkness of the night sky.

Down below, they could see an Elf looking nervously up a ladder.

“I don’t think he wants to go up there,” Mr. Grit said. “And he really will wish he hadn’t shortly.”

Crook glanced at Mr. Grit and then peered back down over the lip of the ridge. He squinted at the Elf, and then a wave of recognition washed over him. “Why, that’s young Evergreen!”

Mr. Grit broke his gaze away from the Elf, who was now nervously starting to climb up the ladder, casting his eyes down the ground every few seconds, and looked down at Crook.

"Evergreen?"

Crook nodded, then gulped. Perhaps, he thought to himself, he had said it with a little too much excitement. "Yeah, Evergreen — that's the name of the Elf who's climbing the ladder. Evergreen Frostly."

Raising his thin hand to his even thinner face, Mr. Grit began to scratch his pointed chin with his pointy fingers. "And just what can you tell me about Evergreen?"

Gulping again, Crook fiddled with his fingers. For some reason that he couldn't explain, he felt nervous — nervous to share any information about Evergreen, nervous about being back here in the North Pole, nervous about being a part of the ply to bring down Father Christmas. He had been bored of the North Pole when he had been here, and he had felt so free on the day of his Banishment. Nothing, he had thought, made him happier than being able to go to the City and do what he wanted, when he wanted, and with who he wanted — and Mr. Grit had seemed a great person, and his plan had seemed to be a great one, too.

But, now that he was back here, it all seemed so far-fetched.

Somewhere in that crowd down there, Crook thought to himself, would be his twin brother. His Mum and Dad might be there, too. His whole family.

Now he was turning against them — truly turning against them, even more so than he had done before, but this time — well, this time, if it was found out that he was a part of what he and Mr. Grit were about to do, then he would never, ever, ever, be able to return back to the

North Pole. It would be unforgivable beyond unforgivable. He gulped at the thought.

"Goblin!" snapped Mr. Grit. "I just asked you a question, and so I expect a response. I shall ask you again — what can you tell me about Evergreen McFrostly?"

"He's a new Elf in the business," Crook replied, seeing that he had no choice but to reply. "If I remember correctly, then this will be his first Christmas working for Mr. Claus. His Mum and Dad have worked in the industry for a long time. If I be honest, I'm surprised he's a Star Elf. I don't think anybody in his family — or, at least, for many generations — have been chosen to be the Star Elf of the Year. It would have come to a big surprise for them." Then, thoughtfully, Crook added, "Evergreen must have been a really good Elf this year. The Committee don't usually pick Elves so young to be the Star Elf, especially with the height that the trees are starting to get. It's dangerous."

The longer Crook had spoken, the more squinted Mr. Grit's eyes had become. Crook had been too engrossed in what he had been saying to notice, but now that he had stopped talking he looked up to Mr. Grit, and immediately gulped for the third time in just as many minutes. Mr. Grit did not look very happy.

"You sound," Mr. Grit started, leaning in to Crook's face, lowering himself down to the ground, "as though you are almost impressed by this Elf. Or, as it would appear to me, as though you are concerned about this Elf. And, it would appear to me," Mr. Grit continued, a nasty look flickering across his face, "as though you're having — how to put it — *second thoughts*."

Crook shook his head vigorously from side to side. "No, no, no, Mr. Grit!" he exclaimed. "I can promise you that is not the case."

"Hmm," scowled Mr. Grit. "That better not be the case, otherwise you'll be packing your case. You hear me?"

Crook nodded. "Understood, Sir."

"Good," Mr. Grit nodded. "Now, let's do something about this Elf."

With that he stood up quickly, spun around, threw his hands up into the air, his long, pointed fingers raised up to the darkness of the night, and then he launched them forward.

Ripples appeared in the air, the same way as the air above the ground wobbles on a hot day in the middle of the summer, and waved towards the Town Square.

Crook shot up and looked over the ridge, and he saw the ripples reach Evergreen, and then he saw Evergreen let go.

And down he fell —

Down.

Down.

Down.

Till he reached the ground and the thud echoed through the Town.

Mr. Grit cackled, swept his hands through the air once more, and then they were gone.

8

THE CANDY CANES immediately fell quiet, and so did the crowd. They all just stood there, watching and waiting, in shock, for Evergreen to move.

It had all happened so quickly. One moment he had been at the top of the tree, about to pull down the star, and the next he was falling, falling fast and yet seemingly in slow-motion at the same time, until he had hit the ground and a horrible thud had rolled through the Town Square.

"Nobody panic," Goose said, taking over the megaphone and speaking to the audience. "Everybody just stay where you are until we can get this situation into order."

Mr. Jingelton looked lost and confused, unsure of what he should do. It was a good job Goose was there to be able to take over the situation. Without wasting another minute, Goose put his hands into the air and start waving them around, in a rhythmic action, circling them around and around in a circular motion. Around the base of the Christmas tree, and the stage, and the small, crumpled body of little Evergreen, gold particles rose into the air around them all and then joined together, expanding into both directions until all the particles joined together to create a small golden dome over them all.

"There," Goose said, proud of himself, but a serious look drawn across his face. "That will give us some privacy." All sounds of the outside audience was blocked out, and the only people inside the golden dome was Evergreen, Goose, Mr. Frederick Jingelton, and Father Christmas. "We can't hear them and they can't hear us. Nobody will be able to walk in, but we'll be able to walk out." Overhead and all surrounding them the golden dome glimmered and shimmered. It would have been a pretty sight to spectate if it hadn't have had to be conjured under the circumstances that it had been.

Goose rolled his sleeves up, then scurried over to Evergreen, getting down on his knees and observing him. "I just don't understand how it happened," Goose said, shocked. "Nobody has ever just fallen off the tree before. We've spent years upon years testing that ladder."

Mr. Jingelton raised his eyebrows. "Testing the ladder? I just thought a ladder was a ladder — and anybody could fall off a ladder."

At this, Goose turn around and looked up to Mr. Jingelton, obviously shocked at the fact that he could presume such a thing. "Excuse me if you think I'm speaking out of turn, but do you really think I'd be so silly as to let any old Elf go off climbing up a ladder that just gets taller and taller year after year and not put safety precautions into place, hmm?"

Mr. Jingelton looked as though he was about to argue back for a moment, but then he must have thought better of the idea, because instead he just clamped his mouth shut and shook his head from side to side. "No, no," he muttered. "I don't."

"Well. Good," Goose said, a little too quickly. He must have been expecting Mr. Jingelton to argue back with him and seemed a little disheartened at the fact that an argument didn't seem to be coming his way.

He cleared his throat and then continued speaking. "THAT ladder had spells put upon it," Goose began to explain. "Nobody was supposed to be able to fall off the ladder. Heck, I didn't even think anybody could fall off the ladder. That was the whole point of it!" As he spoke, he waved his hands up in the air frantically. He really wasn't very happy. "Even if young Evergreen here thought he was about to fall, he would have been stopped. Subconsciously, the ladder makes you keep at least one limb on a rung or the side of the ladder at all times. We've had Elves and Goblins try to fling themselves off it for weeks now, and no matter how hard any of them tried, not one of them were able to do it. Not one!"

Goose's face began going red, and he continued to wave his arms manically in the air, as he was still on his knees, kneeling down next to Evergreen. Outside of the golden dome, the rest of the crowd continued to wait and watch, but all they could see was Goose's mouth moving and no words coming out of it, because of the sound barrier. Whatever it was that he was saying, they thought, he looked as though he had a lot to say about it.

"Just think of the audience!" Goose said. "Think of what they will say, what everybody will be thinking. This whole thing has been a shambles — they'll never want to come and watch an Elf put the star on top of the tree again. Nobody will ever want to be nominated as the Elf of the Year."

Then: "Maybe we're going to have to cancel this event in the future. I should have known we were being too ambitious, too silly, striving to make the tree as tall as it is — I mean, we all know it's not natural! We all know it's bewitched!" He let out a moan. "That's it," he said. "Christmas is over. Christmas is ruined. Christmas is done with before it could even get started!"

Father Christmas bolted forward at this, shaking his head side to side, his great white beard swinging from the left to the right and back again. "No, no, no, Goose!" Father Christmas exclaimed, seemingly horrified at this suggestion that Christmas could be cancelled. "I simply won't hear anything as crazy as that! This is just a small blip — we'll manage to make everybody trust us again. You don't have to worry about that.

"At the end of the day," Father Christmas continued, kneeling down besides Evergreen and joining Goose, "all that happened is a small accident. Evergreen fell off the ladder. That's it. People fall off ladders all day, every day, all over the world."

Goose shook his head. "No, no, no," he said. "It's not as simple as that. This isn't just about Evergreen falling off the ladder. It's about…" he paused and took a deep breath.

"About what?" Father Christmas said, pressing Goose to speak.

Mr. Jingelton kept quiet, stood at the sight and watching on. He could feel the eyes of all the crowd watching him intently, looking at them all, desperate to hear what was going on, growing impatient to find out just what had happened.

Everybody knew it was impossible — should be impossible — for an Elf to fall off the ladder. Everybody was going to want to know why it happened and how it happened, and what they would do to stop it happening again, and how they would make sure it would be prevented from happening again. He could hardly focus on it all — trust something like this, something as big as this, to happen when he was Head Elf. The amount of work and PR he was going to have to do now was beyond all imagination. He was already beginning to grow worried that he wouldn't be able to pull it off. Father Christmas was bound to have high expectations as to how they should all manage this; he would want them to work a miracle, and Mr. Jingelton just wasn't sure whether he was capable of it. He was going to lose his job over this, he thought to himself. All that time wanting to be Head Elf and now he was going to lose it all, all because somebody had fallen off the top of a ladder. It was Goose's fault, he thought to himself. If Goose hadn't decided to make the tree as tall as the tree was, then maybe this wouldn't have happened. Only Goose was to blame for this.

"It's about the bigger picture," Goose said. "There's more to this than meets the eye. The spells that have been used on this ladder have been used for years — no Elf has ever fallen off. It should be, theoretically speaking, impossible to be able to fall off it. The only way this could have happened..." he paused, his eyes wide, clearly horrified of what it was he was about to say. "The only way this could gave happened is if somebody did this."

"If somebody did this?" Mr. Jingelton said, unable to keep himself quiet anymore.

"That's right," Goose said, nodding, his eyes widening and his mind racing. "Somebody who knew just what to do and just at the right time. Somebody... somebody who would want to cause injury, cause confusion, cause mayhem."

"But why would somebody want to do that to Evergreen?" asked Father Christmas.

"I don't think it's about Evergreen," Goose replied. "It's just a sad fact that it just so happened to be Evergreen who had been chosen by the Committee to be the Elf of the Year and was up the tree."

"Maybe it was somebody who had something against Evergreen," Mr. Jingelton suggested.

Father Christmas nodded, scratching his beard. "That's a possibility. Do you know anybody who had anything against Evergreen?" he asked. "Perhaps someone who might have not been happy at the thought of Evergreen being named the Elf of the Year? Somebody who would want to sabotage it?"

Goose shook his head again. "No, no — definitely not. Evergreen is a good worker — it's only been his first year this year. He's good, kind and happy, and everybody likes him. I think you could scout this town from top to bottom and you'd struggle to find one person who didn't like him. No," he continued. "This could have happened to anyone."

“So what are you saying?” Father Christmas asked. Mr. Jingelton turned to look at Goose. They both waited for an answer.

Goose gulped for the third time, then spoke:

“Someone among us is trying to bring. Down. CHRISTMAS.”

9

EVERYBODY INSIDE OF the golden dome didn't know what to say. Goose looked anxious, more anxious than anybody had ever seen him before, even when the workload and the pressure of making sure everything within the North Pole was done on time and ready for Christmas was piling up all around him.

"What do we do next?" Mr. Jingelton asked him.

"I'm not sure," Goose replied, "but for now I think the best thing we can do is to get Goose to the hospital. We need to get him looked at and make sure he's okay."

"Agreed," said Father Christmas, his eyes darting over Evergreen. In all this time, he still hadn't moved and was still laid out limp on the floor. Every now and again he would do a small shudder, a nerve juddering his body. "He can't be left much longer."

"I'll take him to the hospital wing," Mr. Jingelton announced. He went to un-do the golden dome and scatter the shimmering particles.

Goose startled, jumping forward immediately. "No!" he exclaimed.

Mr. Jingelton turned around on the spot, nearly jumping in the air. "Blooming' hell, Goose — you nearly gave me heart attack then! What's the problem?" he asked.

“The crowd,” Goose said. “The crowd can’t know what’s going on. If anyone asks, just tell them we’re investigating but that it appears to be some error with the ladder. Nobody can know that there’s someone — or something, for that matter, — trying to bring down Christmas. Do I make myself understood?”

Mr. Jingelton’s thin cheeks started to blush red. “I’m sorry, Goose, but may I just stop you and remind you just who it is that you are talking to. The last time I checked, I was still the Head Elf around here. I don’t need to be spoken to like that.”

Goose glowered. It was obvious he was unsure of how to respond.

On one hand, he knew Frederick had a point — whether he liked it or not, whether everyone knew or not just how much Frederick relied on Goose, to everyone else Frederick was still the Head Elf.

But, on the other hand, Goose knew Frederick did not stand a chance without him, and he knew that Frederick needed him.

Deep down, Frederick knew this, too. He knew that if Goose decided to today quit the job, call it the end, then it would be the end of Frederick and the North Pole. Then everything really would be a mess, and — right now — that was both the last thing he wanted or needed.

Father Christmas just stood, awkwardly, looking between the two Elves. He let a moment or two pass, and then he cleared his throat.

“Um… Evergreen,” he said.

Goose and Frederick pursed their lips, then broke off their stares at one another.

“Of course, of course, Sir,” Frederick said, and then he took his hands from his side and raised them in the air in front of him. He wiggled his fingers, sliding his hands above Evergreen, up and down, and then lifted his hands slightly. In time with his hands, Evergreen began to levitate, lifting up from the ground until he was several feet above the ground.

Frederick kept one hand outstretched, guiding Evergreen to a gentle stop, then with his other hand raised his ElfSpeak device closer to his mouth.

"Goblins," he started, raising his voice and talking in a more serious tone. "I need you all to make a pathway from this dome to the hospital. Evergreen here needs immediate attention. Don't say anything to the crowds — just get them separated. Understood?"

"Understood," grunted a Goblin back, in a deep voice.

'On your command, Sir," came the voice of a second Goblin, this one much higher in pitch.

"Thank you," replied Frederick. He dropped his ElfSpeak, then turned to face Father Christmas. "I'll take him now. I'll leave you to say something to the public."

Goose had to try not to roll his eyes. Of course Frederick would volunteer to take Evergreen to the hospital — it made him look like he was doing his bit and got him out of the way of having to do any of the real work. Goose had always prided himself in being an Elf that was usually calm and collected in any and every situation, but for some reason right now with Frederick he was finding himself getting more and more annoyed with the whole thing. If it wasn't because of just how much he cared for Evergreen, the Elves, the North Pole Village, Christmas, and his duty towards Father Christmas, he would genuinely be considering just walking away right now and seeing just how well Frederick would be able to function without him, but he didn't want to let down Father Christmas. As far as he was concerned, his duty towards everything else needed to outweigh his spout of annoyance towards Frederick. He swallowed away his annoyance, and then clapped his hands all of a sudden.

The golden dome burst like a bubble would after being pricked by a pin, and the particles shimmered away and fell to the ground in a flash. The coldness of the air outside rushed into the space and came biting back at their skins, and the sound of the watching audience whooshed back in quickly, like the rolling of a wave breaking onto the seashore.

"What's happened?" came the voice of one Elf.

"How's Evergreen?"

"Did the ladder throw him off?"

"Is someone against us?"

"Is he breathing?"

"Is he dead?"

"Stop, stop, stop!" called out Goose, quickly getting to his feet and marching over to the microphone on the stage. "If we could all just follow the lead of the Goblins, please, and split into two. We need to get Evergreen to the hospital and we would really value your co-operation and your assistance with making sure he gets there as quickly as possible."

The audience did as they were told, and Frederick turned on the spot and Evergreen, still levitating in the air, was raised higher still and then began to be taken through the middle of the crowd, Frederick following several feet behind him, his hands outstretched ahead of him.

Goose watched until they had gotten through the crowd and then disappeared out of sight out of the Town Square, then looked down off the stage, out and over the crowd.

Nobody looked as though they were going to be going anywhere anytime soon. People wanted answers, and he knew he had a duty to provide them with as much information as he could — but the problem was that some of the information he didn't want them to know yet, and the biggest problem was that there were hardly any confirmed information to be able to give them in the first place.

For the first time in his career, he was completely unsure of what he should do — and he didn't like that.

He looked across to Father Christmas, who gave him an encouraging nod and offered him a small smile. "You've got this," he mouthed.

Goose pursed his lips and chewed the inside of his mouth, then looked back out at the crowd, and began to speak.

"Tonight, we had something happen that has never happened before..."

10

"WHAT DID YOU say that for?" Father Christmas yelled. "I've never heard anything like it!"

Goose closed his eyes, trying to keep himself together. "Nobody told me what to say!" he argued back. "I just told them what I thought would be the best to say!"

Father Christmas massaged his temples, then rubbed his eyes, before walking across his office and taking a seat behind his desk. They were back at his grotto, where he and Goose had frantically rushed to as soon as Goose had finished his short speech to the Elves, informing them what had happened and attempting to cover it up. They didn't want anybody knowing anything or worrying over nothing until they themselves knew just what was going on.

"You should have just said we didn't know anything yet, not tell them it's us who's made an error, Goose."

Goose went to say something back, to argue, but then he sighed. He knew Father Christmas was right, but that still didn't mean he had to be happy about it.

"At the end of the day," Goose protested, "it is us who made the error. If we find out it is from someone who's tried to cause trouble, then it's our fault for not picking up on them and for not putting procedures in place to act as a prevention to a situation like this one. If we find out it wasn't caused by anything at all, then it's our fault again because it means something went wrong with either the tree, the ladder, or the star. Either way, it all boils down to us, Sir. It was our event, and that means if something goes wrong during it, then we are responsible. Is that not the way it should work?"

Placing his boots on the surface of his wooden desk and leaning back in his chair, Father Christmas sighed and rested his hands atop of his stomach. "Sometimes, Goose," he said. "Sometimes. But until we know for sure I think it's best if we don't say anything at all. If we say anymore, it looks like we haven't got control on things. I've been around here a long time — a very long time, the truth be told — I know a lot and I've seen a lot. Trust me when I tell you I know what I'm talking about."

Goose was stood at the other end of the office. The office was a cosy room, circular and all made out of wood. There were grand bookshelves running around the room. There was a ladder cast sleek wood with gold feet in the shape of reindeer hooves that, by the looks of it, could slide along the shelves to allow access to the books higher up. The ceiling of the room was very high.

On the other side of the office was a large map of the North Pole — it was like a blueprint, except instead of blue paper and white ink, it was black paper with gold and silver ink, making it look even more impressive and important. It was full of little scribbles, dates and arrows. Just one look at it and it was obvious that Father Christmas was a man who knew the workings of the North Pole inside and out; he knew the date that everything was happening, and he knew where everything was, who was where and when and what they were doing.

The floor, in style with the circular shape of the room, looked like the inside of a tree trunk if you were to cut the tree in half and look at the remaining tree stump. Great big rings could be seen spilling out in all directions from the centre of the room and across to the outer edges of the sphere. It all helped to give the impression that you were inside of a some huge tree. It was incredibly cosy. Nobody else in the rest of the North Pole had a room quite like it. A big fluffy rug, a smart grey colour to match the colours of the rest of the room, was laid between the desk and window.

Goose was stood by the window, which was also round. Outside, looking down, he could see the final few people that were left of the crowd from before stood about talking, slowly making their way home, the last trickles from the ceremony leaving the Town Square and nestling back into their cottages for the night. The North Pole, after all, was a working town with early starts and places to be when the morning rolled around and the sun came up — nobody had any reason or any desire to be staying out for very late on a nighttime.

Looking out over the town, Goose felt a type of responsibility — he felt responsible for these people, for their feelings, for their worries, their welfares, their well-being. He knew sometimes he didn't always do what was deemed to be right in the business-world, but rather did what was right for the people — after all, he felt that that was his job to do so, even if sometimes it did seem to get him into a pickle. He wouldn't have it any other way. No, he thought to himself, he *couldn't* have it any other way. That was just the type of Elf that he was, and he couldn't help that. If anything, that was what made him so passionate, what made him get up in a morning, what made him work so hard — he believed it was this that had helped him to become Deputy Head Elf, and he believed that was the reason why he wouldn't want to be Head Elf. As Head Elf, you couldn't be so much about the people — not if you wanted to please people as high up as Father Christmas, anyway, and that, he had decided long ago, wasn't for him.

Of course, now, Father Christmas was not a bad person. Father Christmas was a good person. But, at the end of the day, what is important to remember if you're working for Father Christmas, is that even if it isn't to make money, Father Christmas was essentially the head of a business. A very magical business, that did very magical things, and in a very magical place, but it was a highly complex thing to do — there were seven billion people on the planet, and less than twenty four hours to deliver billions more presents. Operating for that many people and trying to make the entire world happy was a very tremendous task, and one not to be taken lightly. It was this that — quite understandably — meant that sometimes Father Christmas had no choice but to be a bit harsh from time to time, and think about what it was that was shared with the rest of the Elves. He needed to maintain control, and make sure everything was kept in order — one day of things going wrong— heck, even one hour of things going wrong! —

and everything would be affected, the backlog and the consequences would be… well, they would be unthinkable. Just the mere thought of it alone sent shudders down Father Christmas' spine and had kept him awake back in the early days, back when he had been new to the job.

No. Father Christmas knew what he was doing — but he realised that Goose needed to know more.

"I'm going to tell you a story, Goose," Father Christmas said, "and I need you to pay attention. Okay?"

Frowning, Goose pulled himself away from the window, turning his back to the snow that was beginning to fall outside, drifting outside heavier and heavier from the sky. "Okay."

"Take a seat, please," said Father Christmas.

Goose did as he was told, padding across the office and sitting in the chair on the other side of Father Christmas' desk. The chair was smaller than Father Christmas, which looked like a small throne, but it was still a plush purple and silver.

"I'm going to tell you about my third ever Christmas, after I had taken this job. Now, nobody really knows much about Father Christmas — everybody thinks they do, but they don't. For starters, everyone on the outside world seems to think I only work in December, the one month of the year, or — even wore — just Christmas Eve, and we both know that's not the case. But they don't know that. They think I'm overweight, have a big belly, and — well, I guess I can give them that one, because they have kind of got a point there." He shifted in his chair and looked down as his stomach wobbled about a bit. He sat up and pushed his glasses further up his nose, then rested the palms of his hands back down on his desk, and continued speaking.

"But they don't know what happened with Christmas before me. They don't know about my childhood. They don't know what I do in my spare-time, or the food I really like to eat, or what it was like for me growing up. They probably don't know — as you probably don't know — that it was my father who did this before me. When Mrs. Claus and I have start having children, it will be my son — or daughter, now that I've changed the rules and it's been accepted by the Committee— who will take over the running of Christmas, along with their wife or husband, whoever either of them are happy with.

"Anyway, I'm going off topic here — as I was saying, nobody really knows. But many, many years ago, when it was my third Christmas and I was working with all of your great-grandfathers and great-grandmothers, we had a Christmas that ended up being a big disaster, and I mean *big*."

At this, Goose sat up in his own chair, listening carefully and shuffling forward to make sure that he wouldn't miss a word.

"Why?" he asked. "What happened?"

"For starters, we had the worst weather imaginable. A furious storm like no other I had ever experienced. But on top of that, it was the day before Christmas Eve when things started to go wrong. Up until then, everything had been running like clockwork. Not so much as a small blip.

"Out of nowhere, we had an infiltrator break into the North Pole.

Nobody expected it and nobody knew what to do. It was the first time it had ever happened, and my father had died during the year of old age, hence I was relatively new to the job and I had nobody to ask what to do. The alarm was raised, which resulted in the North Pole being put under shut-down. I wasn't allowed to leave the North Pole until we found out what was happening and who had broken in.

"In the end, I decided I would take a risk. I thought I knew best and I thought I knew what was I was doing, but I was wrong. The reindeer and I got several hundred feet into the air when the reindeer suddenly faltered. Before I knew what was happening, we were hurtling down to the ground, The reindeer got injured, and sadly some of them were told they were never be able to fly again. I, too, was seriously injured, and there were nothing they could do to get me better in time. I was late in delivering the presents, seen as a bad new leader, and at the same time Christmas was cancelled and it caused confusion and upset the whole world over. People thought I had done a poor job, and they wished for nothing more in the world for my father to be alive. Now just imagine how that would have felt, because of the simple fact that they thought you were incapable to do a job of which you had been raised to do and was your destiny to fulfil."

Goose shook his head side to side. "I'm sorry to hear that, I am."

Father Christmas bowed his head. "Me too." He took a deep breath, then continued with his story. "The first few months of that year were terrible — the world was upset, faith was lost in Christmas, and faith was lost in us, as the North Pole, and faith was lost in me. I don't know which one felt harder to deal with — people not believing in the North Pole or me. I felt a duty to everybody out there to do well and to prove to them I could do the job well, and if people stop believing, then it makes Christmas begin to die a slow death, and I guess I felt as though I was the one responsible for that if that ended up being the case. But, most importantly, on a personal level, I guess, I felt as though I had let my father down. I had wanted so, so desperately to make him proud, to show him just what I could do and what I was capable of doing. He left behind big boots to fill, and I had been sure I could fill them."

Listening intently, Goose took it all in. "Then what?" he asked. "What happened next?"

"I found out it wasn't my fault," Father Christmas replied, lowering his voice as though he was still being listened to, even now, all these years later.

Goose gasped in just the right place. His timing was perfect to help Father Christmas in his telling of his story. "Who's fault was it?"

"That," Father Christmas replied, "is still a mystery, even to this day. All I know is this: one day, just after Easter, after four months of feeling I was the worst thing that had had ever happened to the North Pole, and after I had considered leaving, giving it all up, a note came through the door. It was a black envelope — sleek, and stuck shut with a silver-stamped emblem. For ages, I tried to research who the emblem represented, but I was never able to find out. All it had on it was an eagle, and that was it."

"What did the letter say?" Goose asked. He was lost in the story now.

"That I wasn't to blame. That somebody had purposefully tried to sabotage Christmas, tried to bring the reindeer down, that they had something against my father and wanted to try and seemingly get revenge back by taking it out on me. Whether or not they knew my father had died, I don't know the answer to that."

"The letter came from the person who did this?" Goose questioned. "What made them change their mind?"

Father Christmas shook his head. "They didn't," he answered. "The letter wasn't from the person who did it. The letter came from a person who had figured it out — they must have hunted down this villain, and brought an end to it, found out what had been going on in the process and the villain's reasoning behind it all, and then written me a letter in the process explaining it, telling me that I didn't have to worry anymore. That it was all over."

Goose nodded. "That was that?"

Father Christmas bit his lip and bowed his head. "And that was that."

"Nothing else ever happened?"

"Nothing else ever happened," replied Father Christmas. "Not for all these years — years upon years. That is…" he said, lowering his voice again and sounding grave, "…until tonight."

Goose swallowed. His head felt as though it was swimming from everything he had heard. All this time he thought he knew about everything that had gone on in the North Pole — but little had he known about these threats from the outside that the North Pole had faced. They had always been kept quiet, and the thought of it ever occurring had never crossed his mind. He had assumed everything was happy, that everything was peaceful, and that everyone loved Father Christmas, the Elves, the North Pole, and everything that went on here and everything that they did. The thought that some people out there seemed to be against them, seemed so intent on bringing them down, bringing Christmas to an end and tearing down everything they had worked on so hard for all these years, filled him with dread and made his stomach feel as though he had swallowed a great big lump of coal.

It was only now, now that Father Christmas had shared this story with him, that he was beginning to piece two and two together, and realise just why Father Christmas didn't want to say anything to the crowds that had been watching outside. The North Pole needed to stay a happy place. They didn't need to know that. Father Christmas didn't want them to know. He wanted, more than anything else in the world, to keep the North Pole a happy place — Goose knew that Father Christmas felt as though not only would he be letting himself down, but also as though he would be letting his father down too, if the North Pole fell unhappy. He simply wouldn't allow it. In his mind, he simply couldn't allow it. It was out of the question.

"Do you think it's the same person?" Goose asked. "After all these years, come to return and try again?"

Father Christmas shrugged his shoulders. "Who knows? It could be. They could be coming back to finish what they started. But I don't know — I don't even know who saved us the first time round, let alone who was the villain, if that's what you'd like to call them."

Goose puffed up his cheeks, and for the first time he noticed just how strained Father Christmas looked. His eyes looked tired and the veins on his face seemed to be bulging. His cheeks had seemingly lost their usual rosy-red that blushed them up, and he looked pale. For the first time, Goose realised, he was seeing Father Christmas expressing his true, real concern — and he had never seen it before.

"I think I just need some time to think, if you don't mind," Father Christmas said, sinking further down into his chair.

Wiping his forehead, Goose nodded. "Certainly, certainly…" He pushed his chair back and then stood up to his feet.

As he walked across the office and reached the door to leave, he heard a sigh leave Father Christmas. Goose turned around, and all he could see was the back of Father Christmas slumped behind his desk.

"Father, Sir…" Goose said, quietly.

Father Christmas didn't reply.

"It will all be okay," Goose murmured. "It will all be solved in the end."

"I know it will," Father Christmas said, barely audible. "I know it will."

Goose stood at the door for a moment, unsure of what to say next, then decided it would be best to just say nothing at all. He exhaled, then turned on the spot, and walked out of the office, closing the office door behind him.

11

MR. GRIT AND Crook took off across the North Pole, running as fast as they could.

Across the snow they ran, storming through the icy, miraculously not slipping.

"What's next?" Crook croaked, his voice sounding slimy and greasy as they ran.

"We cause chaos," cackled Mr. Grit. His long legs meant he could do great, big strides as he ran, poor Crook struggled to keep up. If he had been a nice Goblin, and not one who prided himself in helping a villain to succeed in his villainous acts, then you would have almost have felt sorry for him.

"How?" questioned Crook.

They stopped running. Mr. Grit turned to face Crook. Crook looked up to Mr. Grit.

"You," said Mr. Grit, simply and sternly.

"Me?" asked Crook.

"Yes!" exclaimed Mr. Grit. "You! That's what I said, isn't it?" He waved his arms about, getting cross, at an alarmingly fast speed. "You're going to go back to the North Pole."

Crook's eyes immediately opened, so wide in shock that they

looked as though they were about to fall out at any moment and go rolling across the snow. “What? I… I can’t do that. I can’t do that, Mr. Grit, Sir. I haven’t been back to the North Pole for years.”

“Well, then it’s about time you returned, then, isn’t it?” snarled Mr. Grit.

Crook looked across, confused. “I can’t remember agreeing to this,” he said.

Mr. Grit threw his hands up in the air and then lowered himself down to Crook’s level. “Yes. You. Did.” He said, his chin seemingly more pointy than it had been before, and the circles under his eyes like huge shadows across his face making him look more scary under the light of the moon, making him look extremely pale and milky white, resembling a ghost. “You agreed to it the moment you agreed to help me in this mission. If somebody is going to help me in succeeding in a mission, then they’re agreeing to do whatever it takes to make sure I am successful. So, Goblin, you will go back to the North Pole, and you will do what I say, I will take down Christmas, and I shall be successful.”

His eyes glinted. “Now,” he continued, pursing his thin lips, “do I make myself clear?”

Crook had no option but to nod in agreement.

“Good,” snapped Mr. Grit, and that was that. He raised his hand in the air, spun on the spot, and then he was off sprinting across the snow again.

Crook cast a glance back at the North Pole Village, in the distance behind him, then sighed. Then he turned back around and made off across the snow after Mr. Grit.

He knew he had no choice but to follow him. He was beginning to question just what it was that he had managed to get himself into…

12

WHEN EVERGREEN FINALLY awoke, he was terribly confused.

He was in the hospital wing, he knew that for certain, but as for the reason why he was in there, or how long he had been in there for, he did not know.

Looking around, he could see that he was in a hospital bed with a green duvet and a white bed frame. The walls were a clean white and looked sterilised, but they were beginning to light up pink from weak sun rays that spilled in through the window. It was either sunset or sunrise, but which one it was he didn't know that, either. He tried to remember what had happened to him, but the more he tried to rack his brain, the fuzzier everything seemed to get. He seemed to remember some sort of a fall, but from what it was that he had fallen from, he couldn't remember.

Leaning back in his bed, he suddenly realised just how sore he was feeling. A bandage had been wrapped around his head, and so supposed he must have sustained some type of injury to his head. His back felt a little numb, and his knees ached — where had he fallen from? It must have been very high up. He felt as though he had been in a collision with Santas sleigh.

He shuffled around, attempting to make himself feel more comfortable in the hospital bed, which was beginning to feel more and more lumpy the longer he spent in it, the door to his hospital room opened and an Elf walked in, with long brown hair and golden looped ear-rings that looked big enough for a parrot to be able to sit on. She was wearing a blue pinnifold with a white apron tied around her. She must be the Nurse.

"Good morning, Evergreen," the Nurse said with a smile. She appeared very bright this morning. "How are you feeling today?"

Evergreen attempted to smile back, but even his face seemed to ache for some reason. "Morning," he muttered, discovering that his voice was hoarse. "I'm a bit sore today. Is it morning? Or evening? I'm afraid I can't quite tell."

As she busied herself pouring him a glass of water and making up some porridge for him, mixing in milk with some oats, he squinted at a name badge that was on her pinnifold. "I'm Nurse Lavender!" it said. "I'm here to make you better!"

"It's morning," Nurse Lavender replied. "Half past six in the morning, to be precise," she added. "I know, it's early to wake people up, isn't it, but that's what time we need to start our rounds. There' are more Elves falling sick in this North Pole than there is time, and with Christmas coming up and what with it being the busiest time of the year, we can't really hang around in what we do. We've got to make you are as better as we can, as quick as we can, don't we! I'm sure you'll be eager to return back to work."

Everything that Nurse Lavender was saying seemed to develop into a vortex inside Evergreen's head, and he began to find it difficult to process one thought at a time. It was like trying to catch a hundred balloons all at the same time that had been released in the middle of a hurricane. It just didn't seem to be possible.

"The North Pole?" Evergreen asked.

"Yes," smiled Nurse Lavender. "That's right — you don't have to worry; we didn't have to transport you to another hospital. We're quite the specialist here when it comes to falls and bumps to the heads."

At least, Evergreen thought to himself, this one explained what had happened to him. He had fallen, but from what he had fallen from — well, that was still a mystery.

"I mean, the height of that Christmas tree — no wonder you've ended up in here for two days! I think anybody would have been knocked clear out cold from that height. They're getting so dangerous with how big they're starting to bring those trees in. I'll be interested to see what they do next year, now that this has happened with you." The whole situation seemed to be getting Nurse Lavender quite angry, because as she finished talking she pursed her lips with a little 'Hmph!' and slapped a metallic spoon into the bowl of porridge a little too forcefully, sending a blob of porridge onto the duvet on the bed.

Nurse Lavendar's cheeks immediately illuminated red. "I'm terribly sorry," she said, and hurriedly got to mopping it up with a cloth she drew out of her pinnifold. "I just get so annoyed sometimes when they try to put on a spectacle and impress people in front of health and safety and just pure common sense. Here's your porridge, Evergreen."

Evergreen took his porridge with a quiet, mumbled thank you, but he found more and more questions bubbling up in his mind with every second that passed him by.

"Who's 'they'?" he asked, after a couple of silent mouthfuls whilst deep in thought.

"Father Christmas! That Head Elf! That blooming Goose! The lot of them — sometimes I just don't know what they're playing at. Now eat your porridge up before it gets cold." and with that, Nurse Lavender bustled across the room to sort some flowers out in a vase on the windowsill, then walked back across the room and out the door, vanishing from sight.

Poor Evergreen felt as though he had learned nothing. Goose? Who the heck was Goose? Had Nurse Lavender meant a literal goose, as in a bird? But then she had spoken about the top people running the place — running the North Pole, he was sure she had said — and there was no way a feathered bird could help to run a huge organisation like that.

Evergreen shook his head from side to side, and then returned to his porridge. He ate the rest of it quite peacefully, feeling sure that he must still be unconscious, and that all of this with Nurse Lavender talking about geese and the North Pole was just some weird type of dream he was having, and that he would wake up soon or be told that some sort of a joke was being played on him.

Enjoying his porridge, he decided, was the best thing for him to do for now — and so that was exactly what he did.

13

BEHIND A SCREEN in the corner of a dark room, illuminated by one dull naked bulb that hung from the ceiling, Crook was looking at himself in the mirror. He sighed. He really didn't like what he saw reflected back at him.

"Hurry up," came a voice, grunting, and Crook rolled his eyes.

"Mr. Grit, Sir," he said, "I really don't think this is a good idea."

"Why?" pressed Mr. Grit.

"I just don't think it is," Crook said back, attempting to sound normal.

"Let's see you," Mr. Grit said.

"I don't think —"

"I said, let's see you!"

Crook shook his head and then shuffled from behind the screen and into view of his boss. Mr. Grit immediately began to applaud.

"Oh, Crook!" he bellowed, clapping his hands together and slapping his knees, hard. "I don't understand what the problem is! I think we're onto something here." He cackled again. "This plan is going to go down a treat!"

But Crook really wasn't too sure, and as he returned a weak smile to Mr. Grit, he looked down at his body and what he was wearing, and he had to try not to cringe. He was wearing what he used to wear back when he worked in the North Pole — he looked like an Elf version of a candy cane, all red and white stripes. He had pointy shoes on with bells at the end, red and white stripy tights, and a green jacket on. On the top of his head he wore a green hat with a red bobble on the top of it, and he felt like a Christmas tree, all red and green and decorated.

"You look great!" exclaimed Mr. Grit.

"I look stupid!" bellowed Crook.

Mr. Grit shook his head. "Well, then you'll fit in with the rest of the stupid lot, won't you?" He cackled again, this time at his own joke. "So what if you look stupid — you didn't come and work with me to look nice and feel pretty! This is taking over the North Pole we're talking about here! Bringing down the festivities, bringing an end to Father Christmas — not walking in a fashion show!"

At this, Crook's cheeks illuminated red. Not that he was usually bothered by what people said to him, or — at least — he liked to think he wasn't — but when Mr. Grit tried to make him feel stupid he didn't like it. Instead, it had the opposite effect.

"What do I need to do?" he asked, more determined than ever. Not only did he want to show Mr. Grit he could do it, but he wanted to show him that he could *really* do it well — to prove Mr. Grit wrong.

"Come with me," Mr. Grit said, his voice low and slimy, "and I'll show you."

14

FATHER CHRISTMAS SUNK his face into the palms of his hands with a long, deep sigh, and stayed that way on his desk for a couple of minutes, until there was a knock on the door. For a moment, he attempted to ignore it, hoping that whoever it was would change their minds and leave him alone, deciding that whatever it was they wanted to talk to him about wasn't really that important.

There was a second knock on the door, and Father Christmas pulled his head from his hands and rubbed under his eyes. Shadows were appearing, creating circles underneath them, and his temples on either side of his head weren't feeling too great, either. He felt as though he had a lot of pressure around his brain, a sign of all the pressure he now felt he was under.

This time of year, in the run up to Christmas, was always busy, as to be expected, but this was something that he had never predicted. One simple act of Evergreen the Elf falling off the Christmas tree, and everything had spiralled out of control in a way that that he had never even imagined. The Security Goblins bombarded him with message after message, hour after hour, convinced that there was some sort of evil force from the outside that had caused this. Father Christmas said that he was open to the idea of it, accepted and agreed that it could be a possibility, but he still thought it was something to do with the ladder — that it hadn't been bewitched and — or, even — tested properly.

The Department of Bewitchment and the Department of Security didn't like this at all, and neither did the Department of Testing. They made it clear they had done their best, done what they had done every year to make sure that nothing out of the ordinary could happen at the Christmas Tree Ceremony.

"We've been doing it for years!" grunted the Head of Security Goblin, Bart. "If I didn't know how to run an event as huge as this one then I'd have found myself handing in my letter of resignation a very long time ago, Sir, if you do excuse me! Now I'm telling you — the person who is responsible for this event is someone evil, someone with huge motivation behind them, and someone who none of us could have expected. I mean, and I don't mean to brag," Bart continued, puffing up his chest and re-arranging the collar of his blazer, "but myself and my Security Goblins are some of the best — if not, I'd like to argue, the best — Security Goblins in the whole world. If someone had gotten past us, then it's someone we've got to worry about."

His words had stayed with Father Christmas, and they had been ringing in his head ever since. "If someone had gotten past us, then it's someone we've got to worry about…got to worry about… got to worry about…"

A knock at the door came for a third time, this time louder and harder than the two previous knocks, and Father Christmas was startled out of his trance.

“I’m coming, I’m coming!” he boomed, flying up from his chair, sending it rocketing backwards behind him, and marching over to his office door.

With an almighty yank, he pulled it open and then looked down.

It was Goose.

“What now?” Santa said, almost at a shout. A few Elves and Goblins who were working nearby looked up, shocked. Father Christmas’ red cheeks blushed a little redder than they usually were, and he cleared his throat. “Sorry, Goose, sorry.” He said, this time with his voice lowered and trying to sound kind. “How can I help you?”

Goose, however, looked nervous, and appeared to be struggling to stand still.

“Goose?” Father Christmas said, his thick, white brow furrowing. “What is it? What’s happened?” he asked. He had seen Goose stressed and worried before, but he hadn’t seen him act quite like this.

Looking around, Goose leaned into Father Christmas, and Father Christmas knelt down slightly. “Can we talk in private?” Goose asked.

Father Christmas stood up straight again. “Of course, of course,” he said, standing back and outstretching his arm into the air, gesturing for Goose to come into the office. “Come in, come in.”

Goose walked past him and into the depths of the office, and Father Christmas stuck his head out of the door and looked up and down the corridor. A couple of Elves and Goblins who had been looking from their work to Goose and Father Christmas at the office door, muttering between themselves about what could be going on, saw

Father Christmas looking at them and hurriedly looked away again, taking a newly-found very, very big interest in their work and falling silent, their cheeks all illuminating so red that between them all that Father Christmas was sure they could have powered the entire North Pole Village for a week from the heat radiating from them.

He chuckled to himself, shook his head side to side, then stepped back into the office, closing the door behind him, and wandering back over to his desk.

"So, Goose," he said, "what's the problem?" He resumed his seat behind his chair, and looked expectantly at Goose, who was sitting on the other side of it, looking anxious.

Father Christmas then noticed that Goose was holding some papers in his hands, that were shaking and rustling as Goose fidgeted anxiously.

"What are those?" Father Christmas asked.

"What are what?" Goose said, looking about.

"Those!" exclaimed Father Christmas. "You know what I'm talking about Goose, you don't need to play silly with me — you and I both know that you could run this North Pole single-handily if you had to, so don't mess around."

"Right you are, Sir, right you are," and then Goose appeared to loosen up a little. "I've come to show you something."

"Presumably whatever it is are written on those papers," Father Christmas said.

"Well, yes, Sir. That would be correct, Sir. But—"

“Pass them over.”

“But what you’ve got to—”

“Pass them over, Goose.

“But what you’ve got to understand that I have nothing to do with this. Nobody else wanted to show you because they were too nervous, but they’re too important. They could be damaging, and whilst I don’t like having to come to you to show you these, from a business point of view I feel I have no choice but to.”

Father Christmas nodded. “I understand. Now, I would like to have a look please.”

Goose nodded. “Certainly, Sir. Certainly.” and he passed them over to Father Christmas, who began to read:

THERE HAS BEEN a lot going on in the North Pole as of recent times, and it’s become worrying. For those of you who don’t know what we, at The Northerly Herald, are talking about, then you’d need to count yourself lucky, because you’ve obviously been on a very nice vacation away from around these parts.

Just 3 nights ago, a young Elf, Evergreen McFrostly, was selected by the Committee to be the Star of the Year, the Star Elf. This, as everyone knows, is an incredibly special honour to be awarded, and it is a hugely important part of the Annual Ceremony of the revealing of the tree that takes place in the North Pole Square every year, on December the 1st.

Usually, everything goes to plan, but this year something

went wrong. Hundreds, if not thousands, of Elves had to witness young Evergreen dramatically fall from the top of the tree, and fight for his life.

A golden dome was created around Evergreen, with Father Christmas himself and his team within the half-sphere. No information was given immediately, and crowds were forced to wait until any news was broken, with many of the spectators attending the evening fearing the worst.

"You just don't know in these type of situations," said one Elf, Miss. Angelica, who's son is also an Elf who works for Father Christmas. "Usually news in this place is provided for us quickly, but in this case we heard nothing. Of course it makes you think something terrible has happened." Miss. Angelica went onto add that she "feels terrible for the family of Evergreen and she can't imagine what his poor mother must be going through."

The Northerly Herald has made an attempt to get in contact with the family of Evergreen for a comment on the situation, but as this article was going to print we are yet to hear anything — and the same can be said for Father Christmas too. With no update regarding Evergreen, nor any sightings of him, indicating he may still be within the depths of the Hospital Wing, as well as no official updates from Father Christmas, Mr. Frederick Jingelton, or any other members of the Head Team or Committee, it is fair to say that the public of the North Pole are beginning to grow ever concerned as to just what really happened

on this night, and just what might the North Pole Team be covering up.

Edwina Inksmith, reporter for The Northerly Herald.

Father Christmas slammed the newspaper cutting onto the surface of his desk, and looked up, poor Goose trying his best to hide from view.

"Who let this be printed?" he asked, demanding an answer. But all Goose could do is shrug. "I don't know, Sir," he admitted. "I wish I could help you, but I can't. The Northerly Herald is a newspaper that hasn't been running for very long — they're fully registered, but they're an independent newspaper. They run on their own — they don't have to print stories that are approved by us. Some would say, I suppose, that they're not always pro-North Pole."

Shaking his head side to side, Father Christmas looked as though he couldn't quite get his head around this fact.

"But what for?" he stammered. "What would be the point of that?"

Goose let out a sigh. "I'm afraid," he said, "that times are changing, Sir, and with that so is the demand for news. As society continues to grow and develop, so does the type of news that they wish to consume. People don't always like to trust one newspaper — and it's for that reason that we need to start worrying."

Rubbing his temples again, Father Christmas grunted and then leant back in his chair. He dropped his hands from either side of his head and then put his fingertips of both hands together, his elbows resting on the surface of his desk, as though he was deep in thought.

"I guess," he said, after a moment of quietness, "it is just one story. Just one story. That's what we have to remind ourselves of."

Goose nodded. "That, Sir," he said, "is very true, but even one story can be enough to spark something bigger. We're going to have to get thinking and acting on this, and quick. After all, Sir, in all due respect — if we are being realistic — we haven't really given the public any true answers or explanations, have we?"

This, Father Christmas knew, was true.

"I know, I know," he admitted, "but…" He trailed off.

An expression of concern washed across Goose's face. He could see that Father Christmas was worried. "What is it, Sir?"

Father Christmas opened his mouth to speak, then closed it again, then opened it once more. "Because, Goose, I'm clueless. I do hate to admit it, but I am. I have no idea what happened — even the Security Goblins don't know what happened." He then looked around anxiously. "And… and I've fallen out with them."

Goose sat up in his chair, a frown etching the top of his face. "What do you mean," he asked, "that you've fallen out with them?"

"Well…" Father Christmas started, and then he fell silent.

Goose shook his head. "No," he said. "I'm sorry, Sir, but I need to know what happened. I can't deal with things going on, things like that," he gestured his head at the newspaper cutting, "if I don't know just what it is we're dealing with."

Father Christmas sighed. "I know, Goose, I know. But, that's the thing — I don't know what I'm dealing with, what we're dealing with. The other day, when I was having a meeting with the Security Goblins, they seemed to think that the thing, that the reason, as to why Evergreen fell off the top of that Christmas tree is because of outside reasons."

"Outside reasons?" echoed Goose.

"That's correct," Father Christmas confirmed. "Nothing internal."

Goose scrunched up his face, trying to follow what Father Christmas meant. "I'm… I'm not sure I follow what you mean."

"What I mean, what the security goblins mean, is that someone or something who is not a part of the North Pole jeopardised the Christmas Tree Ceremony and harmed my Star Elf of the Year. They believe it's some evil force who's behind this. But I'm just not sure I believe them. I tried to, I tried to think whether it could be a possibility, but I… I just don't think I can."

Goose listened, and then he kept quiet. For a moment, neither Father Christmas nor Goose said anything to one another, falling into silence so that nothing except for the hustle and bustle of the North Pole around them could be heard, the workings of the Elves and the Goblins as they busied themselves in the preparations and the productions for Christmas.

"Please correct me if I am wrong in what I'm about to say, Sir,"

Goose said, talking quietly and slowly. "But when you say you're not sure you think you *can't* accept it could be a possibility, do you mean you really *can't*, or…" He took a deep breath, because he knew what he was about to say next was risky, because it could be taken the wrong way. "Or that you *won't*?"

For a moment, Goose thought he had gotten it all wrong, that he had blown his chances of ever being promoted to Head Elf, that he had ruined his chances of continuing to work for Father Christmas full-stop, that he would be sentenced to a Banishment Day, because Father Christmas looked as though he was going to argue back with him.

But then, Father Christmas seemed to stop in mid-track of whatever it was he was about to say, and then he let his head drop with a big sigh.

"No, Goose," he said, and for the first time since they had started working together, for the first time since any of this had gone on, Goose heard tiredness in Father Christmas' voice. Tiredness and stress and concern, and Goose began to grow concerned for Father Christmas. He wasn't too sure anybody else was. "No, Goose, you're right. You're completely right. I don't want to accept that anything or anyone has ruined this. I've spent my whole life working for this, my whole life making the North Pole what it is, that I can't bear the thought of anyone trying to just come along and ruin it, and especially not as easy as they have supposedly already done so. I mean, that ladder has been worked with for years, and worked on by some of my best people who I would trust with my life. If even their tricks, their spells, their bewitchments, can be imposed and thrown over, then what else could this… could this … could this THING do. The thought of it — well, the thought of it just fills me with shudders. I can't bear the thought of it. Can't bear it, Goose."

Goose suddenly felt sorry for Father Christmas. Goose knew he had spent years himself working his way up through the ranks, had worked his way up to becoming the Deputy Head Elf, and he had — whilst obviously being in love with the North Pole and all the work they did, all that they stood for — tried his very best to be able to achieve, but he felt as though along the way he had forgotten just why he started out. He felt as if he had lost true sight of what they were doing, the reason as to why they did it all, and it had all become business to him.

But for Father Christmas?

Well, this was his life. This is what he had worked for — this was way more than just a business, more than a promotion. This was his livelihood — in his blood, in his bones, in his family. From generation to generation, this is what his entire family had done, and this was, for want of a better word, his destiny. Doing this — running the North Pole — was what he had been born to do.

The more Goose thought about it, the more he began to think about just how Father Christmas was feeling. Not just the stress of having to do everything that normally went on throughout December, but also dealing with this — dealing with the PR — dealing with the public, their questions, their concerns and their accusations — and dealing with his own personal feelings.

Goose decided to take on a chance, and say something to Father Christmas.

"I hope you don't mind me saying something, Sir?"

Father Christmas looked up from his desk, where he had found himself staring into space, and shrugged his shoulders. "Certainly."

"This isn't your fault," Goose said, "and you don't need to feel responsible for it. But I know you will and I know you do, but you don't have to. We're in this together, and we'll solve this together, and we'll get to the bottom of it together. You're not alone. You don't have to feel as though you've let anybody down, because you can trust in me when I say you haven't. You haven't let us down as workers, you haven't let those out there down," he gestured outside of the window towards the Village that splayed out below, "as the public, and — most importantly — you haven't let yourself or your family down. That's a fact. You hear me, Sir?" he said, speaking louder now, his voice filled with more confidence. "That is a fact, a promise too. A promise from myself."

Father Christmas looked up from his desk to observe Goose, and Goose offered him a small smile.

"I mean what I say, Sir. We will sort this out."

Father Christmas smiled back. It was a weak smile, but it was still a smile, and that was all — if not more — that Goose had been hoping for. "I know we will, Goose. I know we will."

Goose's smile grew into a grin. "That's what I like to hear! That's the spirit, Sir."

That was when Goose noticed that Father Christmas' eyes were looking glassy, because he had the hint of tears in them.

Secretly, Goose's words had touched Father Christmas, and for many years to come Father Christmas would always remember them.

For a long time, if Father Christmas had been honest about how he felt, he felt as though he had just become a necessary part of Christmas — as though it was often forgotten that he too was a person. Yes, admittedly, he was magic, but just in the same way that having lots of money didn't always mean that the richest man in the world was the happiest man in the world, the most magical man in the world wasn't always the happiest, either. So, Santa thought to himself, it was nice to be seen as a person again, even if it was by his Deputy Head Elf.

"Thank you, Goose," he said.

"For what, Sir?" Goose asked.

"For everything," Father Christmas replied. "For just being you."

Goose broke out into another smile. "Why, thank you, Sir."

"Now then," Father Christmas exclaimed, standing up from behind his desk hastily and clapping his hands together. "Come on, Goose! We have work to do!"

He grabbed a feathered quill and a scroll of paper, and got to work.

Goose giggled and joined him. They knew they had no choice but to fight back, and time was of the essence.

15

EVERGREEN AWOKE AGAIN, unsure of what time it was or what day it was. He felt as though he had been in the hospital for ages, and he was ready to leave. He wanted to go home. Nothing appealed to him more than going back to his home and back to his own bed, rather than this hospital one which was seeming terribly lumpy. Nothing appealed to him more than going back to his own and getting to eat his porridge, which would be nice and warm with honey and sugar on top, rather than the hospital one which seemed to be cold, milky oats not mixed in together very well. Nothing appealed to him more than going back home and being able to go back to work, rather than just sitting here, laying with nothing to do, time tick'ing and tock'ing him by.

More than anything else, Evergreen just felt terribly bored.

Just as he sat up to try and make himself comfortable in his bed, there was a knock on his door. Evergreen frowned and looked across to the door. Nobody had knocked for him for ages. The doctors and the nurses just seemed to walk right on in whenever they wanted to do so. This meant, he thought to himself, getting excited, that he had a visitor.

The knock sounded for the second time.

"Come in, come in," Evergreen exclaimed, running his hands through his hair and trying to neaten it up, being the messy, fuzzy, bed-head bird-nest that he thought it was.

The door opened, and in walked an Elf, and Evergreen felt his heart drop. He thought the guest might have been somebody who he worked with, somebody who had come along to see how he was doing, but it wasn't. In fact, Evergreen had no clue who this Elf was.

Yet, at the same time, Evergreen thought to himself, the Elf looked strangely familiar, almost as though he had seen him before, recognised the face, but he just couldn't remember where or recall why. No matter how hard he tried to rack his brain, he just couldn't put his finger on how.

"Good morning, Evergreen," smiled the Elf, closing the door behind him and wandering across the hospital room, past the foot of the bed, and then taking a seat. "How are you doing today?" he asked.

Evergreen frowned. "I'm afraid I don't know who you are."

The Elf shook his head from side to side. "Tut, tut, tut," he said. "Evergreen, Evergreen, Evergreen. Did nobody ever teach you any manners when you were just a young Elf?"

Evergreen suddenly felt offended. "Why yes!" he exclaimed. "Of course I was. I was raised very well, I'll have you know!"

The Elf grinned, but Evergreen couldn't help but feel there were something a little bit odd about it. It didn't look like the happy type of a grin, the nice kind of a smile. "Well, then I'm glad to hear that. I guess I shall have to apologise."

Evergreen frowned again.

"I'm sorry."

"Thank you?"

"You're welcome."

Evergreen laughed.

"What's so funny?"

Evergreen opened his mouth for a moment, then closed it, thinking of what he was going to say, how he could phrase it, but then he changed his mind and thought he would just come out with it. "I just can't help but think you're a little bit strange. And you still haven't told me who you are."

Having taken a seat next to Evergreen's hospital bed, the peculiar Elf suddenly stood up again, cleared his throat, and spoke. "Excuse me," he said, his voice low, almost as though this voice was forced, was hard work for him — something he wasn't used to doing. Evergreen watched as he walked back around the foot of the bed and grabbed the curtain, and then yanked it.

Then he turned on his foot and walked back around to the chair, pulling the curtain with him, until they were concealed from view of anyone else in the hospital. "I just think we need a little privacy, don't you?"

Looking around, Evergreen suddenly realised something wasn't right. He couldn't remember anything like this happening before now, but then — the more he thought about it — the more he realised he couldn't remember very much at all.

"What's going on?" he asked.

The Elf smiled. "I'm Kane," he said. "I'm a new Elf here."

"I think I recognise your—"

"Evergreen," the Elf said, cutting him off. "I'm Kane and I'm a new Elf here."

"Okay," Evergreen said.

Little did he know that Kane was actually Crook. Then Kane smiled again, and leaned in closer:

"I'm Kane, and I'm a new Elf here, and I'm going to tell you a secret."

16

I AM WRITING today an open letter that is written to all of you from myself, Father Christmas. These are my words that I have written — nobody else's, and I urgently ask all of you to listen to me in this letter.

Now I am sure many of you today have heard in the past couple of days the rumour that there is something much bigger going on here, in the North Pole, that I and my team are attempting to cover up. I can promise you this, today, that this is not true. There is nothing we are covering up, or attempting to cover up, because the simple truth of the matter is that there is nothing to cover up.

Within my team here at the North Pole, I place my full trust in them, and if I do, I would hope that you, as the public, would, too. Sometimes, the sad truth is, mistakes can happen. After having discussions with my team, I can confirm that it has been deemed that it was most likely an error with the bewitching of the ladder which enabled Evergreen to fall off the said ladder, and thus become the catalyst of the events that have followed. The "truth" that there is some evil force at work, trying to overthrow Christmas, is simply not true.

I have full faith in my security team, and I can promise you that the North Pole is safe — and if, in the very rare occurrence that we were not safe, then I would ensure that all of you would be the first to know about it. I also have full faith within my team who work with the ladder for our annual Christmas Tree Ceremony — I always have and I always will.

Sadly, now and again, from time to time, mistakes happen. This does not mean the people who worked on the ladder are in the wrong. It just means an accident happened. That, I am afraid, is a part of life, but it is all in the dealings of the mistake — what we learn from the mistake, how we move on from the mistake, and how to ensure that never again is the same mistake made – that is the most important part.

Evergreen, the young elf who fell off the ladder, is safe, happy, and on the route to a full-recovery. That, too, is a promise, and we are hoping that Evergreen will be back to work, just as he wants to be, before we know it.

After all, Christmas is on the way, and is fast approaching. I am sure that many of you will agree with me when I say it, that there is still a lot of work to be done before our annual deadline of December 24th, Christmas Eve, and that we have better places to focus our ideas and our energies, rather than listening to rumours and giving them the attention they do not deserve.

I thank you for reading this today and for listening to me, and I hope that from now on, we can all start to move on, and find

enjoyment in Christmas once more — the enjoyment we all love, and the enjoyment we all so much deserve.

Thank you again and all the best,

Father Christmas.

SIGNED: F. CHRISTMAS.

An Elf with her hair tied up in a tight bun and golden glasses perched on the tip of her long nose looked up from her newspaper, pushed her glittering spectacles back up her face, and sat back in her chair. She dropped the newspaper onto the surface of her desk and put her hands together, her lips tight.

"I don't like it," she said. "I don't know if we can trust him."

A few other Elves and Goblins who were sat in a small huddle of rows in front of the desk nodded and 'mmm-ed' in agreement with her.

"So what do you propose we do about it, Edwina?" asked one of the Goblins who was sat in the front row, in a chair closet to Edwina Inksmith's desk.

Edwina heard the question, but stayed quiet for a moment, deep in her own thoughts. Leaning her head back on her chair, she turned and looked out of the glass window of her desk, which ran from floor-to-ceiling and ran for the full length of one of her four office walls. It was covered with blinds, but right now the slits were open so she could see out.

On the other side of the glass were dozens upon dozens of desks, in a hot and stuffy room. The walls were quite blank, but a few attempts had been made at making the large office feel homely and professional, as a few large plants and palm trees were dotted around the edges in great pots near water-dispensers, but that was about it. They had obviously gone for the minimalistic approach of decorating.

This was the office of the newspapers, The Northerly Herald. It was owned and managed by Edwina Inksmith, who saw herself as the best journalist for miles around.

"I say we find a new story, a different story. I say we find out what they're up to, and we out them. They're up to something," she said, her ear-rings that looked like parrot perches swinging about. "I say I want to be the journalist whose team brings them down."

"It sounds good," admitted one of the other Goblins who was in the audience, "but, if you don't mind me asking, how do you propose we do that?"

Edwina sat up in her chair, and stuck a pencil through her tight hair-bun. "Now listen to me," she said, "and listen to me carefully."

Her audience of elves and goblins shuffled in their chairs and shifted forwards, sitting up and listening intently.

"Now," she began, "we need to get the inside scoop."

"The inside scoop?" asked one of the elves. "What does that mean?"

"It means," replied Edwina, with a grin, "that we're going to find out what Father Christmas is up to, and his sneaky team. I think they're covering something up — as we reported, it could be that some villain or an outside force is trying to infiltrate the North Pole and bring it down. If this is the case, well then the public needs to know this for their own greater good."

"For their own greater good," repeated the elves and goblins, nodding their heads fiercely and triumphantly.

"Exactly," smiled Edwina. "Now, I'm sure you're all wondering just how it is you're going to be doing this, and so I'm about to tell you how."

They all leaned in even further, at this point barely sitting on their chairs, some of them even tipped forward so far the back-legs of their seats were hovering in the air, not touching the ground.

"Some of you will be going undercover. This is a big mission, and I want to make sure it's pulled off exactly how I envision it, exactly how I want it to be done. You'll have very small microphone devices sewn into your clothes — this way we'll be able to hear and record every conversation you have within the depths of Father Christmas' headquarters. Additionally, every morning, when you wake up, till the moment your head hits the pillow on a nighttime, you'll be wearing one of these in your ears."

She raised a hand from her desk and held up in the air a very small peach-coloured dot. It looked nothing more than a small bead, except made out of foam instead of anything hard.

"They're self-charging," Edwina explained. "Like solar panels feed off the sun and have their energy provided for them from the light, these feed off the darkness. Every night, when you get into bed, you need to put these in your shoe or on your bedside cabinet, or anywhere close by you where it can neither get lost by you or be found by anyone else. Every morning, the very moment you wake up, you need to slip it back inside your ear. This way, we'll be able to — very discreetly — communicate with you, and we'll be able to hear you and the conversations you'll be having thanks to the microphones.

"So," continued Edwina, "I've additionally set-up a special office purely dedicated to the ongoing of this task, until its completion. In here, we'll have headsets to be able to communicate with you, and we'll also have our notepads in front of us, we can record not only the conversations you'll hopefully be having, but we'll also be able to document and publicise the answers to the questions that we prompt you to ask. On top of all this, we'll be able to write down not what only you see, but what we see, too — thanks to our latest top-of-the-range technical development of this microscopic camera and video transmitting device."

Edwina put down the peach-coloured foamy ear device down, and then off the surface of her desk picked up a small purple pouch. She pulled opened the drawstrings, loosening the bag, and then slipped her fingers inside, gently and carefully pulling out another small bead, but this one was even smaller than the ear device or the microphone.

One of the Elves near the back row grew so incredibly delighted at this sight and so excited over the mission, he tipped so far forward on his chair that the front-legs of it gave way under him and he went toppling to the ground. Out of trying to save himself, he grabbed the collar off another Goblin and took him down with him, knocking out another Goblin on his way down.

Standing up quickly, the last Goblin grumbled and mumbled and said something rather rude and inaudible under his breath, and returned back to his chair. The Elf and the Goblin he had dragged down began to turn into nothing more than a flurry of arms and legs as they both desperately tried to get back up.

Edwina watched them with furrowed eyebrows and then cleared her throat. All the other rows who had been turned around in their seats to see what all the commotion was, spun back to focus their attention back on Edwina.

"Some of us will be more discreet in this mission than others, I am sure," she said, pursing her lips.

A few of the Elves and Goblins sniggered.

"What's so funny?" asked the Elf getting off the floor.

"What did I miss?" questioned the Goblin as he returned back to his seat, looking disgruntled.

"Never you mind," replied Edwina.

The rest of the Elves and Goblins smirked to one another, then Edwina continued to speak.

"Now, this is a small camera that will be sewn into your clothes that you'll be wearing. It is top-of-the-range, as I've said, and therefore they are not cheap. I do not want any of them broken, and I want all of them returned safely and in one piece upon the completion of this mission. Do I make myself understood?"

"Loud and clear!" chorused her audience.

"Good," said Edwina, nice and simple. "This way we'll be able to report exactly what is truly going on within the depths of Mr. Christmas' HQ."

She smiled at the very thought.

"Now, you're also probably wondering how we're going to get inside. We are reporters. We don't work for the North Pole, we work for The Northerly Herald. We can't break in, because that would raise too much alarm and we'd find ourselves before the Court of the Naughty and the Nice. We can't apply for any work positions, because if they're like anybody else who's looking for Christmas temp, by the time they get around to actually offering you an interview Christmas would have come and gone."

Edwina looked incredibly bitter about this, and the Elves and Goblins briefly caught one another's eyes, looking confused but not wanting to say anything.

"And so," Edwina said, "I have concocted a plan, and — if I say so myself — I think it's a grand plan."

"Just what, if you don't mind me asking, Miss, is this grand plan?" asked the disgruntled Goblin who had been knocked out onto the floor a few minutes before.

"Interesting you should ask, Gordon, interesting you should ask!" Gordon rolled his eyes, but Edwina didn't notice. "One word, guys and girls, one word!"

“And that is?” asked a small Elf.

“Kidnap!”

“KIDNAP!” they chorused back, half-impressed and half-shocked.

“That’s right, folks!” Edwina exclaimed, and then dropped her voice. “Kidnap.”

17

"SHE'S OFFICIALLY LOST it!" exclaimed Gordon. "She's completely gone mad. Mad as a box of frogs. She makes the Mad-Hatter seem normal, and that," he said, raising his hands and tapping his finger in the air, "is an achievement in itself."

"The Mad-Hatter isn't real!" argued back another Elf.

"Oh yes he is, Edgar," Gordon retorted. "I've met him myself, once upon a time. And, if I say so myself, when I left, I thought he was a pretty nice chap."

Edgar shook his head. "And he says it's Edwina that's mad," he whispered, cupping his hand over his mouth and muttering to Willie, another Elf beside him.

The group of them were trudging through the snow. Darkness had once again fallen over the North Pole, and — according to Edwina — this would be their prime-time for getting the mission under way. She had, for reasons unbeknown to the rest of the bunch, trusted Gordon with the blueprints of the North Pole, a sort of map with arrows and squiggles drawn all over it in white ink, instructing everyone where to be and for when.

On the outskirts of the North Pole, The Northerly Herald wasn't close by to the HQ of Father Christmas. The weather had started to become treacherous, but Edwina had still insisted that they needed to leave tonight.

"But we'll get avalanched on!" argued one Elf!

"Lost forever!"

"Never to be found!"

"That's exactly why tonight is the night I want you all to go," Edwina said, smiling, as though this was a perfectly normal thing to say. "That way, if any of the plan fails and any of the Elves get injured, nobody will suspect a thing. They'll all just think it was the conditions and they'll blame the snow. It's a perfect cover-up!"

With these last words ringing in their ears, the Elves and Goblins who had been appointed on this secret mission — excluding some such as the Elf who had fallen off his chair out of giddiness and over-excitement — had been waved goodbye into the snowy, blizzard-filled, night, and been sent off to work.

Now they were about halfway to the North Pole, and considering how long it had taken them to get through the wind and the snow and the coldness so far, the thought of having the same amount of distance to go now was starting to get to them.

"I say we go back!" shouted one Elf.

"No!" shouted Gordon. "We press on!"

"We'll get killed if this storm gets any worse!" argued back another Goblin.

"We're in the exact mid-point!" exclaimed Gordon. "It's the same distance back to The Northerly Herald as it is to the HQ! It's not logical to go back the way we came!"

This, much to the annoyance of a small bunch of them all, was logical and the truth, and — no matter how much they hated it — it was a point they knew they couldn't argue with. So they turned around, with the snow beating onto their faces and getting stuck in their beards. The wind whistled past them, blasts of ice and snow and sleet curling and twisting around them, beating them, the icy blasts cutting across their skin.

For the next mile or so the Elves and Goblins fought against the elements, and by the time they were just a couple of hundred of yards away from the exit of the Father Christmas' HQ, they felt as though they had run out of energy.

"Everyone!" yelled Gordon, waving his hand in the air and gesturing to them all. "Over here! Now!"

"I don't know who he thinks he is sometimes," one Elf said to the other, supposedly under his breath. He didn't do a very good job of it.

"I heard you. I think I have more sense than you. Now come!" shouted Gordon, who was beginning to run out of patience, and the others were beginning to notice.

They followed Gordon, however reluctantly, where they huddled in a bus shelter. They were guaranteed not to be seen here. Anybody who wanted to go out in this weather would have to do so by foot. There was no chance that any buses or cars would be on the road tonight.

"We're here," exclaimed Gordon, "and this means we need to discuss our plan of action. We can't just go in there flailing about, because we'll get caught, so we're going to need to be clever."

He took a large military-style backpack from around his shoulders and flung it onto the floor.

"In there," he continued, "is a dozen or so sacks. We've got a couple spare so they'll be some left over, but we've all got one each. We're going to be going up in two's, one pair at a time. In your pair, each of you will stand out of sight either side of the exit. When the Elf or Goblin you are waiting for — and it doesn't matter who it is, as long as they work for Father Christmas — comes out of the exit, not suspecting a thing, and walks past you and out into the snow, I want the pair of you to run forward, slide the sack over his head, the other one will grab his legs and turn it upside down, and then the first one will tighten the strings and bring back the sack with the caught Elf or Goblin within it."

"And then what?" questioned a Goblin.

"We take his name badge, his hat, his glasses, his uniform, and then we have the disguise. That way, tomorrow, when morning comes, we'll be able to sneak into HQ and carry on their work, as though we are them, and hopefully nobody will suspect a thing."

"Won't people notice we're not them, though?" asked another Goblin.

"Well, no," Gordon replied, in a matter-of-fact tone. "That's the whole point of a disguise. So you are disguised as another person. Disguised means you're pretending to be some—"

"Yes, yes, I know what disguised means," grumbled the same

Goblin.

Gordon threw his hands up into the air. "Well then what are you wasting time for! Edwina gave us this plan and along the way she placed our trust in us. It's not my plan so don't question me on it — it's our job to just do it."

They all stood around, looking at Gordon. He rolled his eyes with a big huff and stamped his foot in the snow, throwing his hands up into the air again in annoyance.

"Well, what are you waiting for?" he exclaimed. "Get to it!"

They all began scrambling about, the huge rucksack being tossed and turned and tugged and pulled this way and that, everyone trying to get a sack out of the bag. Gordon watched the chaos ensue for a few moments, and then rolled his eyes again.

"No, no, no!" he shouted. "Just what do you think you're doing? Give it here."

He marched into the centre of the huddle, grabbed the military bag off the icy ground with a strength that nobody quite knew where it came from, and opened it up.

One by one he withdrew the sacks from the depths of the bag, and began throwing them to each Elf and Goblin. They caught them, and slid their hands across the material. The sacks were rough, like the type you would keep potatoes in. The Elves and the Goblins all agreed that they were glad to be the ones on the other side of the sacks, because they were sure it would be very scratchy indeed being inside of one.

"Right then," Gordon said, once everyone was holding a sack, "is everyone sorted?"

Everybody nodded.

"Good. Do we all remember the plan?"

Everybody nodded once more.

"Good," Gordon said again. "So, we've got a few minutes until everybody finishes. If anybody is a little late coming out then I don't think I'll be surprised considering the weather. They might decide to wait until it passes over. So, Edward and Edgar — you're up first."

The two young Elves, who also happened to be twins, looked at one another. They both looked the same, and yet one looked scared and the other looked excited, and yet they both still somehow managed to look identical. It was strange.

"We can do it," said Edward.

"We'll catch them," called Edgar.

"Right in the sack!"

"And we'll bring them back!"

Gordon nodded. "Yes, yes, yes," he said, brushing them off. "It's all very well reciting poetry—"

Edward and Edgar looked at one another, confused.

"—But there's work to be done, so stop your gabbling and your waffling and get going!"

"Right you are!" Edgar and Edward chorused at the same time.

Gordon shook his head side to side and ran his hands through his beard, and then waved the twins off. They trudged through the snow, somehow bouncing at the same time as though it was easy for the pair of them to move through, almost like the snow was a huge layer of fluffy marshmallow rather than shards of ice and a build up of sleet, and off they went.

"Right then," Gordon said, turning away from Edward and Edgar and looking back to the others. "Time for us to hide. There's some trees over there on the other side of the road. But we're going to have to make sure we can't be spotted, or that we can't be tracked down, either. So," he continued, "I want you all to get into single-file and follow me. I know we all have different sized feet, but I want you all to follow in my footsteps. That way, if someone comes along and looks in the snow, it looks as though just one person has come over here or some wild animal or something else like that — basically, something that won't raise too much concern. Do I make myself understood?"

"Yes, Gordon," they all mumbled back as a collective, long and slow like children do in a school assembly, when wishing the school and their headmaster or mistress a good morning.

Gordon nodded. "Good. Follow me!"

And follow him they did.

Gordon led the way, emerging out of the protectiveness and the covering of the bus shelter, and beginning to cross the road. He looked from side to side, to make sure that nothing was coming, before remembering it would be impossible for anything to be on the roads in a snowstorm like this, and then started walking.

Behind him, another Goblin walked slowly, until Gordon lifted his foot out of the snow, leaving a footstep in the snow behind him, and the Elf placed his foot in the footstep. Gordon then raised his other foot, took a step forward, and made another footprint in the snow. As he then shuffled forwards, leaving another footstep free, the Elf behind filled the empty step again. Behind this Elf, the next Goblin did the same, and behind this Goblin the next Goblin did the same, and so on and so on until they were creating some sort of a weird and slow-moving conga-line moving across the snowy road.

In the opposite direction, Edward and Edgar reached the exit of the HQ and came to a stop, stood on either side of the large archway.

They separated, and pressed their backs against the wall, making sure they were out of sight. They looked forward where they could see the others in their weird line, just vanishing through the trees. Just like Gordon had planned, it looked as though nothing but a wild animal with a slight stagger and strangely-sized feet had wandered from under the protection of the bus shelter and had taken refuge within the snow-covered bushes on the opposite side of the street. Edward and Edgar couldn't help but find it a little bit funny, but they didn't want to say anything to Gordon. They knew he had tried his best to make sure they all were doing what they needed to do, and just trying to please Edwina and make sure the mission was completed the best it could be — and, after all, as they knew very well, as long as you tried your best, then that was all that anybody could ever ask of you in anything that you ever did. Plus, they knew they had a task in hand to do, and so that had to be their biggest focus.

Out of the bushes, they saw a bony hand appear and then — with a quiver and a small dropping of snow over some of the bushy twigs, two eyes appeared followed by a rather large nose and a long white beard. It was Gordon. Edward and Edgar had to try their best not to laugh. It was a very funny sight. It was as though the bush had grown a head and a beard.

He stuck his arm out further and gestured a thumbs-up sign.

Edward and Edgar looked at one another, then back to the bush with Gordon's head stuck out the side, and motioned a thumbs-up back to him.

As though he was a diver, he made an 'okay' sign with his hand, making a circle with his thumb and his finger, and then shook his head from side to side to brush the snow out of his hair and his beard, before vanishing back into the depths of the bush and out of sight.

Edward and Edgar looked to one another, did a thumbs-up to each other, and then shrank back against the brick wall.

It was game on.

18

WITHIN THE DEPTHS of the HQ, steam was billowing out of the tops of machines. Pistons were puffing up and down. Conveyor belts were on their fastest speed, toy after toy after toy being propelled away and sped off to all the necessary departments they needed to be sent away to, to be painted, polished, pruned and perfected over, until they would be ready to be labeled, wrapped and finished with a neat bow, before being dropped into the back of Father Christmas' sleigh, right into the magical sack.

The sack was bigger on the inside than the outside, and although it might be thought that everything would be jumbled up once dropped into the depths of it, it really was magical. If you were to clamber up to the top of the sack, put a foot over the edge, and then drop down inside of it, you'd find yourself in a huge storeroom.

And inside of this storeroom were shelves upon shelves, that went on for rows and rows, stacked up as high as you could possibly go.

There was a ladder that went from the top of the sack and down to the floor, and each row had its own ladder too. On Christmas Eve, some of Father Christmas' best organisers who were great at being efficient, would be employed to spend the night of the twenty-fourth of

December within they sack. In between each stop that Father Christmas would make on his magical and very important journey around the world, the organising Elves hidden inside would be hustling and bustling about, running back and fro, collecting the orders and passing them up to Father Christmas, so that he could easily take them out of the hands of the Elves, pop down the chimney, go into the room of the house he was in, and place the Christmas presents underneath the Christmas tree.

He would then be able to come back up to the sleigh, up through the chimney, and off he would go, onto the next house, and all the meanwhile the Elves within the sack on the back of the sleigh would be busy preparing the next presents.

At this very moment, Father Christmas had finished inspecting the sleigh and the sack, and was now wandering around it, making sure that everything looked okay.

"It looks good to me," Goose said.

"It always looks good," Frederick retorted.

"Not good as in looking good, looks good as in it appears to be safe," Goose said back, a bit more snippy than he probably intended to do so.

"Right," Frederick agreed, nodding his head, although he still looked rather confused.

"Now, now," Father Christmas said, hushing them both. "We've all done this many times. We don't need to argue over it."

"Why?" exclaimed Goose.

"Who's arguing?" added Frederick.

"Because I'm not."

"And neither I am!"

"I never said you were!"

"Good!"

"Good!"

"THAT WILL DO!" shouted Father Christmas, out of nowhere. "Do you think I have the time for this? Well, you don't have to answer, because the answer I have for you is: I don't."

Fredrick looked side to side, eyeing Goose to see what he thought. "You mean… you mean, you don't have the answer or you don't have the time?"

Goose raised his hands in the air in dismay. "What kind of a question is that to ask? You knew he meant the time."

"Well, I was only asking."

"And I was only saying."

"RIGHT!" yelled Father Christmas. He was beginning to have enough. "We have got much more pressing matters to deal with here at this HQ. Evergreen is coming back to work tomorrow and we will need to make sure everything is spick and span for his return — if not, everyone on the outside will be onto us. I'm still unsure what the public are thinking. We still don't know how our newspaper report went down. We still don't know whether it really was the ladder that caused Evergreen to fall from the top of the Christmas tree. So, if you both think I have the time to deal with listening to you two squabbling like a pair of children I would expect to find on my Naughty list, then I am afraid you are both very much mistaken, because I don't. I don't have the time and I don't have the patience."

As he finished speaking, Goose and Frederick looked at one another. Goose gulped. The last thing he wanted was to upset the boss. He opened his mouth and was about to apologise, when Mr. C began to speak again.

"I tell you what, I think I've had enough for one day."

"What do you mean?" asked Frederick.

"I mean I want to send you all home now. I know it's a few minutes early, but I think everybody could do with it."

Goose swallowed. He didn't like the sound of this. Even Frederick, who didn't always see eye-to-eye with Goose on many things, had to agree that this wasn't right.

"Come on, Sir," Goose protested. "We were doing so well when we sent out that report this morning. We don't want to let anyone see we're struggling."

Father Christmas span around. Frederick took a step back. "Who said anything about struggling?"

Goose quickly shook his head from side to side. "Nobody did, Mr. C. I apologise, Mr. C."

For a moment, Father Christmas looked as though he was about to say something back, but instead he just turned back around and started walking to the other side of the room, raising his hands up to his temples. It was beginning to show just how stressed he was getting, and neither Goose nor Frederick liked the sight of it, but neither of them knew what it was they could do.

"You're all dismissed. Thank you to you both for your work today, and thank everybody else too. I'll see you again in the morning for another day of work. Bright and early."

"Bright and early, Mr. C. Bright and early," Frederick said back, but his voice and his words faded quickly to quietness as Father Christmas walked around the sleigh and the huge sack and out of sight, out of the room.

"What's got into him?" asked Frederick, pulling his eyes away from where Santa had left the room and turning to face Goose.

Goose shrugged. "I think he's just a bit stressed. Come on. Let's go tell the others we're closing for the night."

Frederick nodded, and then they both turned on their feet and made their way out of the room and back into the main hub of the HQ, surrounded once more by the dozens of pistons and billows of steam and lanes of conveyor belts, toys here and there, all around to be seen, all in different stages of development, stretching on for miles. Goose and Frederick walked up to a podium in the centre of it all, and Goose picked up a megaphone.

"Ladies and gentlemen, Elves and Goblins!" he called out. Everybody stopped what they were doing and looked up. "We thank you for your work today, but you're now free to go home. We'll see you again in the morning for another day of work. Bright and early." Goose added echoing the words of Father Christmas.

Everybody looked around and then did as they were told, turning the keys in the ignitions in their machines and taking off their goggles, their hard-hats and their high-visibility jackets that were coloured in luminous greens and reds, which matched their helmets. A loud chatter erupted all over the place as they began to talk and get ready to make their way back to their homes together, discussing the conditions outside and how bad the weather had turned. They suspected this might be why Father Christmas had let them finish on time, rather than ask them all to stay on late to work as he so frequently did during December in the run-up to Christmas, when the big night was fast approaching. The humming of the machines, the whirring of the conveyor belts, the whistles from the pistons creating the clouds of steam, faded into nothingness until it was pure chatter and hustle and bustle that filled the room.

A pair of Goblins — Roger and Robin — who worked in the Polishing Department were slipping off their high-visibility jackets as they talked and walked. They lived next door to one another, and so they usually walked home together. Tonight, they were one of the first of all of them to be ready to leave. They often took another exit to everyone else, as they lived more on the outskirts of the Village, and they usually took the bus to be able to cover the distance between the HQ and their homes quicker. Tonight, however, due to the weather, they knew they would have to walk, but this wasn't to be an issue.

"That was a busy day today, Robin," said Roger, running his fingers through his hair. He was slightly middle-aged and Robin thought he had a bit of a look of Albert Einstein to him. He was very intelligent, and despite the fact that Robin often said he could do bigger things within the HQ, such as developing new technical advancements of toys in the technical department, Roger continually insisted that he was quite happy where he was, where he felt he belonged.

"I know right," Robin said. "I think if I were to do any more polishing, I'd polish my hands off!" Robin laughed. She was a younger Goblin, with green eyes and a pretty complexion, complete with long brown hair that she let free now the work was done for the day, but it was usually tied up in a bun and hidden under the protection of her hard-hat. She wore make-up, with bright red lips and rosy red cheeks.

Roger laughed, and then together they made their way out of the exit of the HQ, and into the storm. Together, still in mid-conversation, they walked through the snowy grounds, making remarks concerning the weather and how it had snowed much more than either of them had thought it had.

Then—

WHOOSH!

Everything went black, and before they knew it everything became scratchy and they found themselves separated.

Unbeknownst to Roger and Robin, Edward and Edgar had succeeded.

19

IT WAS EARLY the following morning, and Evergreen was excited to be returning back to work.

He stood back in the mirror, observing himself, and realised he had never been happier to be in his work uniform. He did a small twirl, smiled at himself, then padded through from his bedroom, down his wooden stairs, and into his small, cosy kitchen.

"Morning," he said aloud, although he usually lived alone.

"Good morning, Evergreen," came back a voice, a grin muffling it.

It was Kane.

He was sat at Evergreen's breakfast bar, having just finished a slice of buttered toast and was now demolishing an apple. In his other hand he held a glass of fresh orange juice. He was wearing his uniform that Mr. Grit had given to him. Crook still didn't like it.

"Did you sleep well?" Evergreen asked, politely, whilst busying himself, preparing his own breakfast.

"I did, I did," Crook replied, smiling. "How about you?"

"I did thank you, but…" then Evergreen trailed off.

Crook was just about to take another bite of his apple when he noticed. He dropped his hand and apple, then looked across to

Evergreen.

"But what?" he asked.

Evergreen went to reply, then shook his head side to side, and continued making his breakfast. "No, no," he said, quietly. "It doesn't matter."

Crook shook his own head, placing his apple down into his breakfast bowl, deciding he'd had enough of it, then slid off his stool and walked around the breakfast bar to be in front of Evergreen. He turned him around so he was facing him, so that Crook could look right into Evergreen's eyes.

"If it mattered to you last night," he said, pressing Evergreen to open up, to ensure he didn't miss any information, unbeknownst to Evergreen, "then it matters to me this morning."

Evergreen swallowed. "Right," he said. "Thank you." Then he noticed that Kane wasn't going to let this drop. "I…I just had a dream I was working for Father Christmas, and that I was selected to be the Star of the Year…"

"Yes, yes," Kane said. "That's all true."

"I know, I know," Evergreen said. "But then I had a dream that when I was up the ladder, and it wasn't because of anything I did or anything that the ladder did that caused me to fall off."

Kane suddenly looked worried, but Evergreen was too busy trying to cast his mind back to the dream, back to his fall — which he had only learned had been a fall off a ladder when he had left hospital and a reporter had come up to him and questioned him about it, asked him what had happened, and suddenly that part of the puzzle of what had happened to him suddenly clicked and fell into place within his head. “But, if I remember correctly, I seem to remember having this really weird feeling wash over me. Like, one moment I was up there, then the next something invisible took over me, and then the next thing I knew I was falling.”

Kane nodded along, agreeing with everything that Evergreen was saying, as though he was genuinely taking note, as though he was genuinely being a worried friend. “What you’ve got to remember,” Kane said, being clever with his words when he knew that poor Evergreen could barely remember anything at all, “is that you had a fall. Not just any old fall, but a big fall. It’s bound to happen for some things to be recalled wrong, for some facts to be recollected the wrong way round, for some feelings to be remembered in the wrong order.”

Evergreen chewed his lip, but then smiled a small smile, weak though it was. “I guess,” he said. “I suppose you do have a point.”

“I know I do,” Kane said, grinning, as though he knew he had always had a point. “Don’t let what other people say get into your head, okay? You hear me?”

Evergreen nodded again. “I hear you.”

“Good!” Kane exclaimed. “Now, Father Christmas always makes sure the ladder has the highest security, and on the subject of security, Father Christmas has the best protection team out there that there are in this world. There would be no invisible or outside force that could have done this to you, Evergreen. It’s already been said that experts think it was a mistake what happened with the ladder, and that's all that there is to it. Nothing more. You hear me?"

"I hear you," Evergreen said again, almost as though he was taken in by some sort of a trance by Kane.

"It would take a genius to get past the security of Father Christmas and his Security Goblin Team." Kane said this, then turned back around to leave Evergreen, a wicked smile on his face.

"That's very true," Evergreen said, returning back to busying himself preparing his breakfast, grabbing a bowl out of a cupboard and a carton of fresh orange juice out of his fridge. "If such a genius could do it, as wicked as they would have to be to turn against Father Christmas, then I think I shall like to meet them, for very clever they would have to be!"

"Very clever indeed!" Kane echoed.

Evergreen got halfway through pouring some milk over his cereal, when he stopped and turned around to look at Kane. "Thank you," he said.

"What for?" Kane asked.

"For being there," Evergreen replied. "I don't think we've met before, but I'm glad we have. I think, if I say so myself, you've come at just the right time!"

Kane smiled back. It was a very big smile — but Evergreen just thought Kane was being polite, that he liked the compliment, that he was enjoying his company.

"Me, too," Kane said. "Me, too."

Little did poor Evergreen know just what was going on underneath his own roof.

20

THE PLAN WORKED better than they expected it to.

Before they knew it, Gordon, Edward, Edgar, and the others were stood next to the bushes, surrounded by a dozen potato sacks, which were squirming and fidgeting around, the people they had kidnapped wriggling about in a fight to gain freedom. It wasn't going very well.

Goblins and Elves were good at many things, but if there was one thing that they were truly experts at, it was tying extremely good knots with their small hands — it came in very useful when wrapping bows on presents or trying ribbons around boxes. Therefore, it had been a very easy, useful, and transferable skill to use here.

"You all need to stop shuffling about," Gordon said, calmly and in a low voice, as he stood forward and took the top of a sack that was trying to bounce off the kerb and roll across the road back in the direction of the HQ by the handle and pulled it back. "The more you struggle, the harder this will be — both for yourselves and for us."

"None of us want to hurt you," added Edward.

"We simply want your clothes!" finished Edgar.

A squeal came from one of the sacks. A gasp came from another.

"We're not going to leave you without clothes," Edward said, as though this was the most obvious thing in the world ever, and the people in the sacks were stupid for not thinking about this in this totally normal situation.

"You're going to have our clothes!" Edgar shouted, excitedly, as though this was all a part of a fancy dress party, and everybody should be delighted at the thought of trying on different costumes and imitating different people.

There was another gasp, followed by another squeal. One of the sacks tried to protest, but one of the Goblins picked it up into the air and gave it a firm shake, making whoever it was who was trapped inside of the sack fall silent.

"We told you," the squat old Goblin who had picked up the sack said, "the more you struggle, the harder this will be — both for *yourselves* and for us."

"How is this difficult for you?" said one of the sacks.

"You're not the one stuck in one of these!" said another, the one in the Goblin's hand and still raised off the ground.

The Goblin dropped it back back with a PLUMF!

"Because you're heavier than I thought!" he exclaimed. "It makes my arms tired."

Everyone looked at him. Even though the sacks couldn't see what was on the outside, it somehow even felt as though even them were looking at the Goblin at this point.

"What?" he added, somewhat surprised at the reaction. "I was just saying."

"Enough, enough," Gordon said, amid a circle of eye rolls from the others. "We've had plenty of chit-chat and time is getting on and the weather is getting colder, so we need to sort this out and we need to sort it out quick. So, is everybody listening?"

Everybody nodded and then moved in closer, pulling the sacks behind them.

"So, this is what we're going to do…"

And Gordon leapt into describing to the others their plan of action.

Then, in no time at all, it was all go, go, go.

The Elves and the Goblins were dashing here and there, trying to get themselves sorted, and pulling the sacks into an old building across the road.

"Edwina knows a man who knows a man," Gordon explained, when the others asked about the use of the abandoned building. "She said a bit of this and a bit of that and now we can use it."

The others just nodded along. They didn't know much about Edwina, but they knew enough to know she had a tendency to get her own way. They wondered what it really was she would have said. They were sure it was more than "just a bit of this and a bit of that", but they kept those thoughts to themselves, although they all were thinking the same.

Gordon led the way, dragging his sack behind him, around the old bushes and across a disused patch of snowy land, until they reached the doors of the old building. It was more of an old warehouse than a building, once upon a time used by Father Christmas to store presents, until they created the magical sack on the back of the sleigh, and decided it would be much more efficient to just put the presents in there as they went along, so that they were all in the same place, saving both time, money, and stress.

Pushing against the door of the old warehouse, it creaked open.

Gordon, who knew they were allowed in here, felt nervous, and he never felt nervous. He was the leader of the pack of journalists, after all. He was supposed to be a symbol of strength to the others; he was supposed to be able to put himself into any reporting situation and not let his feelings get the better of him. It was all necessary in getting the best story they could get. Nothing else mattered except the story. That's what he used to remind himself in the past, and that's what he was reminding himself of here.

Except, as he stood back, widening the gap behind the door and the wall to allow the others to file in one by one, dragging their sacks with their kidnapped people inside behind them, even Gordon had to accept that this was the furthest he had ever gone to get a story, that this was the worst crime he ever committed just to be able to publish a good report. As he watched the last Goblin with the last sack file into the warehouse, and as Gordon shut the door behind them and sent them into darkness, he had to admit to himself that — even for the briefest of moments — he stopped and questioned just what it was they were doing — how far would he go for a story? Or for The Northerly Herald — but, deep down, to himself, he knew that the real question he was asking himself was: How far was he willing to go to please Edwina

Inksmith? He wasn't sure that he had an answer, and — on the same token — he wasn't too sure he wanted to know one.

As he shook his head side to side in attempt to shake away the thoughts, he shut the warehouse door and in turn shut out his troubling voices in his head and the enormity of what it was that they were doing along with the snow and the ice and the sleet, and then turned around, and got back to work. The longer he stood around doing nothing, the less preoccupied his mind became, and the less preoccupied his mind became, the more he started to think, and the more he started to think the more he started to regret, and he wasn't suppose to be a person of regret. He didn't like regret. To Gordon, regret was a weakness — and he didn't want a weakness. Right now, he wanted to be strong. He wanted to be seen as strong.

The warehouse was dark, and it looked like an old hangar because it was empty. Whatever the purpose of it was before was a mystery, because any old machinery or anything else that used to be within it had been long gone. A faint dripping sound could be heard in the distance. Drip, drip, drip, it went, making an echoing sound that ran across the warehouse. Gordon and the Goblins usually prized themselves in fearing nothing — out of Goblins and Elves, it was usually the Elfish species that suffered from nervousness more. But there were just something about this warehouse that made their hairs stand up on edge and their skin feel shivery and tingly.

Whatever it was that Gordon wanted them all to do in here, they wanted to just get it done and get it done quick. It was too cold, too weird, too eerie in there to be stood around wasting any time.

Gordon wandered across it, leaving the others in a small cluster for a moment. None of them wanted to move. A couple of them, secretly, wished they were the ones on the inside of the sacks rather than the other way round. Gordon pulled on a short switch, then turned his back on it and made his way back to his team. As he did so, a faint buzzing sound filled the warehouse, and particles of dust floated into the air, as though this was the first time any energy, any sign of life, had been in the warehouse for decades — which was most likely the case. Then bright white light, harsh and clinical, flickered on and off, on and off, throughout the building, long tube lighting illuminating the warehouse up.

The Goblins looked at each other, and even they had to admit they looked scarier than they thought. Under the terrible lighting, which cast shadows under their noses and around their eyes and made them look like ghouls of the night and monsters of the shadows, they looked more like criminals than they were journalists than they thought — and they weren't too sure whether they liked it or not.

Gordon didn't want to allow any of them too much time to think about it.

As if he could read their minds and tell what they were thinking, he cleared his throat and began to talk: "So, as you know, we haven't got much time. The HQ, I am sure, is a clever place — something that none of us, despite our dislike for it, is able to deny. It is likely that they will notice that something is not right at some point — but until that point comes we have a duty not only to The Northerly Herald, to Edwina, but also to the public. We need to be able to find out what is going on and inform the outside world as soon as we can, the best we can, and the most effectively as we can. This means we have to act swiftly.

"Now," he continued, "I know this old warehouse might not be the best of places, but for however long we are on this mission for, this warehouse is going to function as our new home. We're going to take the outfits of these guys and girls in these sacks, and go into the HQ everyday and do a normal day's work, just as Edwina told us to. Tomorrow, after we have the uniforms of these lot, we're going to send them home. We might be able to stay here, but nobody will notice we're missing — but the families and the friends of these all will do so. Therefore, tomorrow morning they're going to go home."

"But won't their families and friends wonder why they're not at work?" one of the Goblins asked.

Gordon raised his hands at this. "Now that, my friend," he said, as if he was delighted that somebody had used their brains enough to think of this problem and enquire about it, "is a very good point. A very good point indeed. Edwina and I spoke about that."

"Send them home?" another Goblin asked. "Well won't that just ruin our plan? They'll just tell everybody back at their homes what we're up to."

"Now if you let me explain, I'll tell you what it is we're going to do," Gordon said, and he seemed to be loving everybody listening to him intently. "We'll send them home, but Edwina provided us with some extra microphone pieces. What we're going to do is insert these microphone devices into their clothes. Their conversations will then be streamed back to The Northerly Herald. In the same department as the department which is focusing on our mission, they'll be a section whose whole focus is purely monitoring the conversations of these people. The moment any of these people break the terms and conditions of the promises and deals I'm about to make to them, then they'll be in big trouble."

"Big trouble?" gulped one of the Goblins. "And just what does that mean?"

"That's none of your concern," replied Gordon. "Even I don't know. It's nothing to do with me, and it's nothing to do with you, either. That's for Edwina and The Northerly Herald to worry about — that's their end of the deal. They look after their side of things, and we look after ours. All we have to do is get these clothes, and do what we've been told. Anything else that happens on the outside I don't want any of you to think about or worry about. It's not our concern. Do you understand me?"

The Goblins looked from one to another, and again there was that feeling in the air that seemed to suggest that some of them felt as though this was all going a bit too far — as though they hadn't thought about just how big of a mission, of a controversy if discovered, they were getting themselves involved with — but they knew it was too late to say anything now, too late to change their minds and back out. They had come this far, and now they knew they had to see it through — and, not only that, they hated to admit, but the more they heard about Edwina and The Northerly Herald and the threats they were making, the more they began to worry whether they would have really had any choice in whether or not they took any part in this. Some of them were beginning to think differently — and Gordon was beginning to realise it. He needed to get them moving, he needed to get this mission underway, he needed to distract the Goblins and he needed to get on with things — and quick. There was no time to waste.

"So, we're all going to sleep in here tonight, and then tomorrow morning — early, to make sure we can all be in the HQ and getting to work within good time in the correct departments, so we don't arouse too much suspicion, although hopefully none at all — we're going to continue putting this plan into action. Has anybody got any questions or concerns?"

Gordon finished speaking and then looked across the Goblins.

"No? Good. Because those who did knew where the door was. Now then, let's get these people out these sacks, give them a bit of fresh air, and then we can all catch a bit of sleep."

He turned around to his sack and began to un-do the knot at the top of it. Behind him, out of his view, the others looked at one another and pulled faces, gulping , swallowing, wincing — the more time they got into the mission, the more they were beginning to question it all. The way that Gordon had just been with them was a side of Gordon they hadn't seen before, and they weren't too sure they liked it.

Nonetheless, they knew there was nothing that any of them could do, so they sighed deeply, exhaling, then turned around and got to work.

They couldn't displease The Northerly Herald.

21

FATHER CHRISTMAS WAS cooling off.

He had found the day difficult. The stress, he knew, was beginning to get to him, and that was starting to bother him more than half of his problems were. He knew he had to look strong, that he had to look as though he had everything under control, and the fact that he knew he was beginning to let the cracks and the crumbles show was something he did not like.

He was sipping a morning coffee and sat at his kitchen table when Mrs. Claus walked in, a stack of newspapers in her hands and an urgent look painted upon her face.

Father Christmas was quick to notice.

“What is it, my dear?” he asked.

Mrs. Claus sat down opposite him at the kitchen table as quickly as she could and slapped the newspapers down onto the surface of the wood. “Look at these.”

Father Christmas put his coffee cup down onto the table and picked up his golden-rimmed spectacles that he had settled down just moments before, to stop them being fogged up from the heat and the steam of his warm beverage, and slipped them atop of his nose, pushing them up with his fingers and then picking up the first newspaper. It was a copy of The Northerly Herald, and he already knew that this much spelled trouble.

He took a deep breath, glanced up at Mrs. Claus, then looked back down at the newspaper, and started to read:

"Rumours have started to swirl around the North Pole that Father Christmas is not a good enough leader for the HQ of the North Pole, and for managing the busy, festive period. It has emerged that Mr. Christmas has refused to comment anymore on the goings-on within the HQ, and has additionally refused to provide any further updates about Evergreen - the Elf who fell from the top of the Christmas tree and ended up severely injured, and subsequently hospitalised for a lengthy duration.

"This had then led to further enquires around Father Christmas. His behaviour is questionable - as a leader, critics have said, Mr. Christmas should be providing the public with the information they need and require. Instead, he has kept us in the dark, and it is beginning to lead the public to confusion and worry.

"The concern felt by the greater public stems from the anxiety when word was spread that the incident on the Christmas Tree Ceremony on December the First could have been influenced from sources from outside of the North Pole — sources that some would have described as villainous. However, with Mr. C refusing to comment it does not help to settle matters, leading the public to question just whether the inner depths of the HQ know more than they are letting on,

or whether it is simply just Mr. C trying to save his Security Team, not wanting to show to the public that sometimes his team can be flawed.

"Finally, a petition has started that has made a suggestion that Mr. C himself be taken to the Court of The Naughty and The Nice in order to have to fully explain himself to the public of the North Pole. Although the petition was only made public in the early hours of this morning, before this paper went to print, it has already had dozens of signatures — in the grand schemes of things, it may not sound like anything to anyone, but from snowflakes grow snowdrifts, and so for Mr. C it very much sounds like a matter to become very worried about, very quickly.

"Edwina Inksmith, The Northerly Herald."

Father Christmas settled the newspaper back down on the table, and then looked up to his wife. She had a sorry expression upon her face.

"I wish I didn't have to show you that, my love," she said, her voice quiet, her tone soft, "but I felt I had no choice. Either way you'd find out sooner or later."

Nodding, Father Christmas looked up at her from his chair at the kitchen table, a grave look around his eyes, his wrinkles showing more than ever. His white hair seemed whiter than it had done a mere few days ago, perhaps even more grey than white, and Mrs. Christmas had to admit she was beginning to get worried about her husband.

"Everything will be okay, you know, my dear," she said,

soothingly. "Everything will work itself out in the end."

But Father Christmas appeared to disagree. "Maybe in the world out there," he said, nodding his head towards the window as though planet Earth and all its population were hovering just outside of it, "but here we don't have the time for things to just work themselves out. We run a big operation, and things need to be kept running smoothly. We need people to believe in us — we run on belief. If people in the North Pole begin to disbelieve, then it will spread. If our own people here don't believe in us, then how we can expect the rest of the world to believe in us all, either?"

Mrs. Christmas' eyes flickered, observing her husband's face, and she felt that was all she could do. Neither Father Christmas nor Mrs. Christmas knew what to say, because they both knew it was the truth. Belief was what the world ran on — you have to believe in things. We believe Father Christmas is real, we believe we can do good in the world, we believe and trust that our friends and family love us. We believe that we are supposed to do the best we can to the best of our best abilities. Without belief, the world would stop turning — the world would become a different place, because nobody would have any hope or faith that people can do good, and the world would freeze and rust up like a cog that has got stuck, and our universe would collapse.

"It's simple," Mrs. Christmas then said, all of a sudden, and to her it was — to her, she realised that sometimes the most obvious of answers were the ones that were the hardest answers to be discovered, because they're right there in front of your eyes. "We need to get people to believe again."

"And how are we going to do that?" Father Christmas asked. He already sounded tired. He already sounded as though the fight was going out of him. He already sounded as though he was giving up — and Mrs. Christmas was not going to let him give up. He would do no such thing, she told him.

"If they want you to go to the Court, then you'll go the Court. We both know that we have nothing to hide — nobody in this HQ has anything to hide, and nobody has done anything wrong. What happened that night on December the First, what happened to poor Evergreen, was an accident and it was a mystery. That's all there is to it — we know that and deep down the people out there will know that. If you refuse, it will just add fuel to the fire."

"They'll just think I'm giving up," Father Christmas said, unsure of what to do.

"No they won't," Mrs. Christmas replied, pulling out a kitchen chair and taking a seat at the table opposite Father Christmas. She patted his arm and took his hand in hers, squeezing it tightly as he looked into her eyes. She wanted to show him, to prove to him, that everything would be okay. "It will show them you're not afraid. That you haven't got anything to hide. That you haven't done anything wrong."

Father Christmas nodded slowly, taking it in. You could almost see the thoughts hurtling around his head, and — if you were quiet enough — you could have almost heard them, he looked so caught up with them all.

"I could do it," he said, then paused for a moment, deep in thought. "I could do it," he said again, "but it would be a risk. A huge risk. If I didn't win, then the Court of The Naughty and The Nice could get me into trouble if they found out I've done anything wrong."

"But you haven't done anything wrong!" Mrs. Christmas exclaimed.

"Iknow that and you know that, but this is a complex business we run. I'm just nervous that they'll find some way to pin something onto me that I — that *we* — haven't done. I don't know why," he continued, "but it feels as though everyone out there has it out for me lately. It's almost as some people want to see me do wrong — as though they don't want me to succeed. And I bet there's more hiding in the shadows. I bet some are under our very noses." He looked, cautiously, around the room, as though it could be possible that one of the culprits could be hiding underneath the kitchen table or behind one of the curtains.

"Now, now," Mrs. Christmas said, patting his arm again, "I think we've had just enough of that. Stop being so paranoid. I say we put out a press notice, and you agree to go to Court — we can prove we've done nothing wrong and that we have nothing to hide. If anything, Evergreen deserves to know the truth."

"Evergreen already does know the truth. He knows we wouldn't do something to harm him — he adores working here. He's wanted nothing more in his whole life than to be able to devote his whole life to our operation, to what we do. You know that just as well as I do."

"I know, I know," Mrs. Christmas said. "And so we need to prove that to those out there who don't believe."

Father Christmas sat in silence. Then he began to nod.

"No," he said, "You're right. You're right! I can't just sit here any longer. We need to find out what happened once and for all, and those out there need to know, too."

With that, he jumped out of his seat, put his red and white jacket back on, leant down to kiss Mrs. Christmas on the top of her head and give a quick squeeze, then turned around and marched out the room, his boots clicking as he went and getting steadily quieter as he vanished out of sight.

A grin spread across Mrs. Christmas' face as she watched him go. Them, with a triumphant nod, she bowed her head, picked up Father Christmas' mug, took a swig from it, then got up.

"Time to get to work," she said aloud, clapped her hands together, and then marched out of the room herself.

She was not going to let the HQ give up that easy.

22

EVERGREEN AND KANE trudged through the snow.

It was a nice morning — bright, airy, and the snow had stopped falling from the sky. Now, it was nothing more than a crisp day. It was still freezing cold, of course, the snow on the ground not melted a bit due to the iciness of the conditions, but all in all it could have been a lot worse, and Evergreen had to admit he was feeling great.

He was excited to be returning back to work. The majority of Elves, apart from the odd one here and there, enjoyed working. Elves always had a lot of energy, and they did not cope well with being cooped up like a turkey in a roosting pen.

Evergreen was no different.

He had struggled with being hospitalised, and stuck in bed, day in and day out. Now, being back on the outside, being back in the real world, he soaked up every minute of the weak sunshine on his skin, turning his face up towards the sky. He enjoyed the slight breeze that passed him by, holding up his hands in the air to allow the wind to curl around his fingertips and brush over his arms. He enjoyed the sound of the snow crunching underneath his shoes and he enjoyed the hustle and bustle as the town around him began to illuminate with life.

As though he had been re-born, he watched as people said

goodbye to one another in the doorways of their homes, waving each other off as they went about their business and on their ways to their respective jobs. He watched as people walked slowly, trying expertly to not slip over on the ice and fall onto their bottoms. He watched as the Road Elves shovelled snow out of the way so that brightly-coloured cars could make their way down the road to take people to places that were further out of town, still to important workplaces, but not in the HQ of Father Christmas.

But, as he watched and enjoyed all this, Evergreen still couldn't shake off the feeling that something just wasn't quite right. He couldn't really explain it, even if he had wanted to, even if he had tried — all he could pinpoint it down to was that it was a weird sensation — a weird sensation that was strong and bizarre and undesirable, unlike any other sensation he had ever felt before.

It was almost as though… Evergreen thought about it, quietly in his own mind, trying to pretend as though he was merely thinking of nothing else at all in front of Kane… but it almost as though everything was *new* to him.

But not just new to him in the sense that he had spent a lot of time in hospital and had missed feeling the sun and hearing the snow and seeing the people of the town, but rather as though this was his first time he had ever been out, as though he was experiencing everything for the first time in his life — and he knew he wasn't. He knew he had been poorly, he knew he had been in hospital, he knew he was happy to be out and he knew he was glad to be able to experience these things again, but he also knew he wasn't being over-dramatic — he knew he hadn't been locked away in prison, or kept in some room at to the top of the tallest tower of a castle for years on end. He had, at the end of the day, he told himself, only been away for a few days — and so why did everything feel so… feel so different?

So strange?

So *weird*?

It was almost as though with everything that he did see, he had to work really hard to process it in his head. He knew his brain had been a lot sharper than this before. For example, Evergreen noticed to himself, when it came to crossing the road at a junction, he knew he had to look both ways to see if a car was coming from the left or right, and yet it took him a moment to realise this. As though it had been wiped from his mind, and then when he had seen other people looking both ways, it had been a foreign concept to him — something he hadn't been able to understand what they were doing, something he hadn't been able to fathom — it wasn't until he had seen them doing it and then seen why they had done it that it all clicked into place, and then the memory had come back to him.

The same had happened all morning to him. From the moment he had woken up, things like getting a shower, brushing his teeth, eating his breakfast locking the door to his house, seeing the snow and everything else had all seemed weird at first, as though he was having to be reminded of how to do them, of how they worked. It was a very strange feeling.

On the side of him, Kane was trooping through the snow too. Evergreen hadn't made vocal his concerns about how he was feeling from his memory after his fall, and it was this that was beginning to concern Kane. He didn't know how Evergreen usually behaved, and so he wasn't sure if the way Evergreen was acting this morning was his typical behaviour or not. But, he reminded himself, that didn't really matter too much — the biggest factor that mattered was whether he would be able to convince Evergreen of something being the truth, even if that wasn't the truth. He knew that Evergreen would still know some basics, if reminded, and this would come in useful — Kane liked to tell himself it was a bending of the truth rather than a telling of a lie.

Kane thought it would be best, he decided to himself, for him to test it out and see if Evergreen was ready. After they had crossed the road, Kane looked up at the sky and saw the weak winter sun.

"The sun should be going down soon," he said, "now that morning is here. The moon usually comes up in the morning."

Evergreen looked up at the sky, too, following where Kane was looking. He could remember the moon, the sun, the day, and the night — these were the basics — but not — unbeknownst to Evergreen — the truth was being bent.

"Oh yeah," he said aloud, "that's a bit odd, isn't it? You'd think the moon would be up already."

Kane smiled to himself and punched the air behind Evergreen's back. He was delighted. The plan had worked. It was all ready to be put into action. He might be able to pull this off. He might be able to actually prove to Mr. Grit that he's capable of doing this right. That he is capable of being trusted. That he enjoyed being trusted.

"Ooh wait," Kane then said, as they crossed another road, the HQ of the North Pole and Father Christmas coming into sight as they rounded a corner. "I got it wrong — it's the sun that comes up in the day, and the moon that comes up in the night." He started laughing. "You can tell it's early in the morning!" he joked. "I'm not thinking right."

For a moment, Evergreen looked confused, and for the slice of a second Kane began to worry that it had been a legitimate mistake, that he had judged it all wrong with Evergreen, that it had just been a mistake because of the early time and a slip of the tongue, that Evergreen hadn't really been convinced about the sun and the moon, the day and the night. But then a different expression appeared to wash over the face of Evergreen, and as it did so Kane felt relief pour over him.

"Ooh yeah," Evergreen said. "Right you are!" And then he continued to walk.

Kane punched the air once more, but then quickly wiped the smile of his face as they approached the gates of the HQ. This was serious business now — he had proven that he could bend the truth with Evergreen; they had managed to get into the HQ, but that had only been because Evergreen had been recognised — then he needed to be clever, and he needed to be on guard at all times. As much as he disliked Father Christmas, the other Elves and Goblins, and the HQ, he couldn't lie about the fact that within the depths of the HQ itself, things were complex. It was a complicated business that Father Christmas ran, and it was twenty-four/seven. Breaking into it and manipulating it wasn't going to be an easy task.

They crossed one more road, entering the shadow of the HQ, the huge building towering above them, and then they both came to a stop outside a pair of wrought iron gates. A guard was stood to the side, waiting for them to approach. Kane began to feel his heart begin to hammer as it finally hit him just what it was that he was about to attempt to do. If he was caught, then this would be the end of it. This would be the end of the mission, and — most likely, he supposed — perhaps the end of him, too. He couldn't imagine how Mr. Grit would react if he had to go back and tell him he'd failed, that he hadn't even managed to get himself into the HQ. If he didn't get past this first obstacle, then the mission would have failed before it had even had a chance to truly get started.

"Morning," said the Guard, tipping his head forward and holding onto the front of his hat. It was like a flat-cap, sturdy but smart-looking. Kane thought he looked rather like the concierge you'd expect to find at a hotel — he was wearing a suit, all black and white — black blazer, white shirt, black tie, black trousers, and black shoes that were so shiny that they were like looking into a mirror. As Evergreen and Kane reached the Guard, Kane looked down at the ground and saw his own face, in the disguise, staring back up at him.

"Good morning," smiled Evergreen, bright as ever.

"Morning," replied Kane, trying to keep his voice down, as though talking quieter would, somehow, make him less visible.

"How are we today?" The Guard asked.

"Right as rain and happy to be back!" exclaimed Evergreen.

"Can I see your Identification Cards?" the Guard asked. "And back from where?" he added.

But he didn't need to ask, because as he looked at Evergreen's Identification Card, Evergreen's name clicked into place, the Guard suddenly recognising it, and then everything suddenly made sense to him.

"Ooh!" he said. "I'm terribly sorry. I didn't know you were Evergreen! You're the Evergreen that fell from the top of the Christmas Tree, aren't you?" he asked. He was so excited about meeting Evergreen and seeing that he was returning back to work, that as he spoke he quickly looked over Kane's Identification Card, barely taking notice of any of the information printed upon it, and passed it back over to Kane without so much as a second glance at the photograph on it, that had been quickly taken and printed by Mr. Grit back before the mission had begun.

Kane quietly exhaled a sigh of relief, and stowed the identification card back into his pocket. It wouldn't be needed to be looked at for the rest of the day now, and if it was the same Guard everyday, then it wouldn't need to be looked at, at all from now on, not if the Guard began to get used to him and recognised him every morning. He wasn't too worried — so many Elves and Goblins worked within the HQ, that new people started there every day. As far as he could remember, the only difficult part was getting in, but he had past experience, and now that he had managed to convince and successfully persuade a member of the Security Team, a Guard, that he was one of them, then the worst part was over. The North Pole was big, bigger than most people thought, and so was the HQ — new people started everyday, Elves and Goblins who had a change of career paths, or wanted a fresh start, or had even come-of-age and had started working for Father Christmas, following in the footsteps of their elder generations of their families. No, Kane decided, he was not worried at all. He knew that Mr. Grit would be very pleased indeed, and that, Kane thought to himself, was the most important thing at all. There were nothing worse than upsetting Mr. Grit and not giving him what it was he wanted.

"That I am, that I am," Evergreen said, smiling but looking a little awkward. Evergreen was, as always, a happy Elf, but he was also a shy Elf. He just wanted to be able to get on with his job and do his part in the HQ — he didn't want to make a fuss, and he didn't want any attention. "I didn't mean to fall off the tree, I should add," Evergreen said, a little laugh clipped to the end.

"We know you didn't, pal," said the Guard, rubbing his hands together to try to get them warm from the cold. "It's all over the papers, isn't it? I don't think anyone really knows what happened, or what's going to happen, either, for that matter."

"Hmm," Evergreen added. "I hope it doesn't cause too much

trouble."

The Guard shrugged, and Kane found himself leaning in closer. He was intrigued. What had he and Mr. Grit, unbeknownst to everybody else, caused? "Some people don't seem to believe Father Christmas when he says it must have been a glitch with the ladder — because that makes people doubt the team who are behind those things. But then if he doesn't say it's that, then it makes it sound like it was a fault of the Security Goblins, and everyone knows that if people don't believe the Security Goblins can keep everybody safe, then everybody will just go into full-on panic-mode for no reason, especially since that would suggest that someone or something on the outside caused this."

"Or, even worse," Kane said, quickly, "someone or something on the inside."

The Guard nodded, chewing his lip, deep in thought. It was obvious he'd been enjoying thinking of all these different theories lately. "True that, true that," he said, "It's a possibility, that's for sure. Either way, I feel sorry for the Mr. C. He's stuck between a rock and a hard place, so to speak."

Evergreen sighed. "I know, and I still feel I'm to blame."

"Nah," The Guard said, shaking his head from side to side and patting Evergreen on the shoulder. "You're not to blame, our kid. It'll be something somewhere that's gone wrong, and I'm sure an explanation that is simple enough will come out soon. We just have to be patient and trust the top guys up there," he gestured within the HQ, "know what they're doing."

Evergreen and Kane nodded, and then Kane looked down at a watch on his wrist. “Ahh well,” he said, breaking up the conversation as casually as he could, “Time is really starting to tick and I think we really must be getting on.”

The Guard tipped his head forward again, clutching the front of his smart hat. “Certainly, gentlemen, certainly. Have a good day — and good luck for your first one, Evergreen!”

“Thank you!” Evergreen hollered back, walking through the wrought iron gates and calling back.

Kane nodded to the Guard in thanks, and then made after Evergreen, not wanting to fall behind. As they walked through the gates, they shut behind them, and Kane felt his heart jump. He had done it. He had actually done it. He had made it inside the HQ. He continued to follow Evergreen as they reached a door in the side of the wall, and Evergreen pulled it open, and then stepped into the depths of the interior of the HQ, and Kane couldn’t believe his eyes.

Evergreen found his own eyes beginning to well up. He was back. He was back at the HQ and he was back to work, and he was back with the people he knew and he was out of hospital and he was returning to doing what he loved to do the most everyday, and there was nothing better than that. Kane couldn’t believe that he was back in the HQ once more — not only did this mean he was halfway there in completing his mission for Mr. Grit, but it was also the first time he had set foot within the HQ since his Banishment Day. It felt very odd, and for the briefest moment he was sure he felt a slight pang of regret, as though he had felt a flash of missing his old life and longing for what it was that he once had. It dawned on him, out of nowhere, unexpectedly, just how different his life was now. He had wanted to leave the North Pole, had wanted to do something different, had wanted to try and carve his own life out, but in that moment as he stepped back into the Headquarters of Father Christmas, in the North Pole, he stopped to think for a moment — just for a moment — if he had really made the right choice.

Then he pushed that thought out of his head, forced it to wash over him and fall away, and then re-focused on the task in hand, remembered how he would feel if Mr. Grit could hear his thoughts right now, and turned his attention back to where he was and what he needed to do. He looked up, re-focusing his eyes to look at his surroundings. The sight of the HQ came flooding back into his vision. For all that he disliked Christmas, for all that he didn't like Father Christmas, for all that he had wanted to escape the North Pole and the life that he had led here, there was no denying the fact that the HQ was an amazing place to be.

It was a huge, open-planned space. The ceiling was far higher than it had looked from the outside, so much so that Evergreen, who was taking the sight all in again after missing it so much from his time spent away in hospital, and Kane both thought that the ceiling just had to have been bewitched to make the room higher on the inside than it was on the outside.

The ceiling was all wooden beams, stretching up into the canopy of the room. The roof was made out of wood, too, and it gave the workshop a cosy feeling, as though they were in a log cabin in the middle of a snowy, ski and snowboarding slope, rather than in what was essentially a toy production factory. From the ceiling was hanging examples and prototypes of different toys — a red toy aeroplane, big enough that you could probably sit on it; an angel with wings the brightest white you've ever seen; a pretend elephant with a blue body and great, pink ears, its trunk raised up into the air happily. All different models and toys ran along these beams, hanging off strings, until they reached the wall on the far side.

The walls were, unlike the wooden roof, made out of brick. They were old bricks, and on one side of the room sloped down to arch over a huge roaring fire, crackling and erupting warmth into the HQ. On the far end, the brick walls met a wooden landing, where Santa's office could be seen, situated in a location where he could look out and down over his workers at any time. On the side of the landing was a curling wooden staircase, meant for the more practical, serious of times, but on the opposite was a yellow slide, twisting and curling all the way down to the ground. Kane wondered whether Father Christmas used it or not.

Next to the yellow slide was a large Christmas tree, a similar replica of the Christmas tree that was located in the middle of the North Pole Town Square outside. This one had fat baubles hanging off, orange, yellow, blue, red and green, draping with tinsel that spiralled around the Christmas tree from the bottom to the top.

On the side of the Christmas tree was a large bookshelf. Some Elf hats were set on the top of it, but running across each and every shelf was book after book, volume after volume. Kane couldn't help but wonder what the books were of, what information they held. Above the bookshelf was a painted oil photograph, set into a large frame in gold. It was of Rudolf the Red-Nosed Reindeer, prancing about in the snow. He looked as though he was having fun.

Looking at the complete opposite side of the HQ, on the opposite wall was a large map, it had all the countries in green, and the oceans in blue. Dozens of strings and pins and post-stick notes were attached to it and running all across it. Even for Kane, who liked to think he was good at trying to understand everything, pretty much admitted defeat when it came to understanding this map. It looked far too complex. If he was to try and make sense of it, make sense of all the strings and notes, then he was fairly certain that he wouldn't know where to start.

Then, in between all these walls and under this ceiling, were the Elves and the Goblins themselves. This was just one room, Kane knew, out of many, within the Head-Quarters, but it was within this one that Evergreen worked, and therefore where Kane needed to be.

They were rows upon rows of desks, all of them messy and untidy and covered in paint, polish and bits of toys. Some toys were complete, piled up and ready to be sent off, but some where in bits, still needing to be put together before they were sent off.

"So, this is the department you work in, too?" Kane asked, trying to sound casual, as he attempted to fathom out what took place here.

"Yeah," replied Evergreen. "We're the Inspection Department — it's our job to do a bit everything really, from health and safety and making sure the toys are working properly and won't injure anybody, to making sure that the paint-work is complete and just looks finished up to a high standard."

"Is that why some toys are done and some are in bits?'

"Yeah," Evergreen said again. "Sometimes we have to take toys to bits if we think there's a problem with them. It's up to us to decide, but either way we need to make sure that everything is okay and finished before we can send it off."

Kane nodded as Evergreen spoke, taking it all in and pretending to actually care. All he needed to know was enough to attempt to do the job himself, and enough to make Evergreen do everything wrong. "Oh," Kane said, "I see. I think I can do that, then."

"You think?" Evergreen said, realising what Kane was saying. "I thought I heard you say you already work at the North Pole?"

Kane looked at Evergreen. "I do," he replied, cooly and calmly. "Department transfer."

Evergreen stayed still for a moment, and for a second Kane was worried that he had — somehow — just gone and blown his cover and ruined everything, but then a smile fell across Evergreen's face. "Well," he said, "in that case welcome to the Department! I'll take you under my wing — we'll get you going in no time!"

Kane grinned back, and Evergreen looked positively delighted at the prospect of having this extra-added responsibility, especially on his first day returning back to the HQ, and Kane couldn't help but feel a little bit bad for what he was doing. It was so obvious to anyone and everyone just how much Evergreen cared for the HQ, how much he enjoyed his work –– but Kane knew he couldn't let some of his own, more personal feelings obscure what he had been sent here to do.

He pushed his own thoughts away, compressing them into a box in his mind and shutting them away, and then clapped his hands together.

"Right!" he exclaimed. "Shall we get to work?"

23

MR. GRIT SAT back in his chair, and pursed his lips, twiddling his fingers before resting his elbows on the surface of his desk, and joining his fingertips together. He looked over them, apparently deep in thought, and then began to speak.

"So," he said, "how did the first day go?"

Crook fidgeted a little in his chair. He was sat on a seat in front of Mr. Grit's desk at an office space he had decided to rent for a bit of time whilst himself and Crook were in the North Pole, "on business", as he liked to call it.

It was more like a dark hotel room than an office — but the ceiling was tall and the windows were narrow, and it was an old hotel. It had no electricity inside of it, and it was lit by the light of candles and candles alone. The building was so old that they weren't allowed to lit fires in the fireplaces, because the heat of the fires might crack the wall structure and damage the building.

This meant that the hotel room was freezing cold, and as Mr. Grit and Crook spoke, inhaled and exhaled, their breath could be seen in the air in small clouds, resembling fog. Mr. Grit was currently sat at his desk, his neck narrow, his back straight, his fingertips pressed together, and looked at Crook with his eyes so piercing, that Crook felt as though he wouldn't be too surprised if Mr. Grit was currently reading his inner thoughts, reading his mind.

"Well?" Mr. Grit asked, pressing Crook for an answer.

Crook shook the thoughts away, and then sat himself up straighter in his chair. "Well," he started, "Today wasn't a great success, if I be honest with you."

Mr. Grit raised his eyebrows. "And just what do you mean by "it wasn't a great success"."

"What I mean is, I tried my best. I mean, I think I tried my best, but he remembers more than he should, Sir!"

"How much?"

"How much what, Sir?"

"How much does he remember?" snapped Mr. Grit.

"Well, he remembers enough that all day today he's been able to tell me how to do the job. He's unsure at first, but then it's as though it comes back to him after he does a bit of thinking. It's almost as though we were nearly there in getting it to work, tampering with his memory, but just not quite enough."

Mr. Grit threw back his hair and jumped to his feet. "This is no good," he said. "The days are passing by faster than ever and we need to start acting fast. Father Christmas won't be hanging around, not now that the public are becoming more scrutinising than ever before. They'll be clamping down on the HQ, they'll be investigating everything and they'll be wanting to know the every goings-on within that place. If anybody catches onto what we're doing, then we'll be in big trouble.

"I know you will, Sir."

Mr. Grit stopped his tracks, and turned to face Crook. "Not just me, you silly fool," he shouted. "Me and you. You and I. We both will. You're in this now just as much as I am. Do I make myself clear?"

Crook nodded quickly, bouncing his head up and down so fast it was a wonder his brain didn't fall out.

"Good," Mr. Grit said, his voice still raised, but then he resumed his walking, stepping behind his chair and wandering back and forth, back and forth, in front of the tall, narrow window. By now the moon was up, and the middle of the night was drawing close. Moonlight was drifting through the window, the night sky clear, and white light cast long shadows across the dark, hotel room, the abnormally tall silhouette of Mr. Grit continuing to move back and forth, back and forth, across the shadows of the desk and the chair and Crook on the wooden floor, the wooden floorboards creaking as Mr. Grit went from one side of the window to the other and back again.

"I think…" Mr. Grit said, his long fingers running along his thin chin, "I think we're going to have to go to Plan B."

"Plan B?" Crook asked. "I didn't even know we had a Plan B."

"We didn't," Mr. Grit admitted. "At least, not at first, but I don't think we have a choice."

Crook pursed his lips. "I'm listening. What's Plan B?"

"Plan B," Mr. Grit said, a cunning smile crossing his face, which made his look even more menacing than he usually did from the shadows and the moonlight criss-crossing his face as he padded from side to side, side to side, "is this."

Eyes following Mr. Grit's thin hands, Crook watched as Mr. Grit stopped on the spot and slipped his left hand into the pocket of his long, black coat, and then withdrew a purple, glass bottle.

"This," he said, shaking the glass bottle from side to side in his hands, the black liquid oozing from left to right within the tiny bottle, "is Plan B."

"What is it?" Crook asked.

"It's a memory eraser," Mr. Grit said. "It doesn't erase every memory, but it does get rid of what we want him to forget," he explained. "Some people use this for their crimes. For example, I once knew a man who was a bank robber. He couldn't break into a bank himself because of the security, but he knew somebody who was an absolute whizz when it came to hacking and security. He told this man, this expert, he would split the money — and it was a heck of a lot of money, we're talking millions here — with him after they had finished their break-in. Anyway, this bank robber slipped the security-hacker this drink, and then after the mission, the drink had its desired effect, and the security-hacker forgot about all the money he was owed, forgot about the bank robber, and all he remembered was that it was him who broke into the bank. He knew he had done it, but he couldn't remember why or how — anyway, the police didn't believe him, but he was arrested and locked up, sent to prison."

Crook gasped when Mr. Grit finished telling the story. "Gosh, he sounds like a nice guy."

"I know," Mr. Grit said. "I knew him. I think he was clever."

"Clever? He framed a man! An innocent person!" exclaimed Crook.

"And now he's a millionaire with so much money you wouldn't even know what to do with it, and literally nobody will ever, ever, ever know it was him who did it!"

Crook shook his head. "Well, I think that's a bit rotten."

Mr. Grit scoffed. "Well, then you go ahead and think it's rotten, but he's got more money than you'll have, and I think you forget this is the villain industry! This is what we do — this is how we make money, this is how we make a living. And you're the one who decided to leave the North Pole and became a part of it. Are you saying now you want to drop out of it? Are you saying that you want to change your mind? Because, Crook, if you do, just tell me now and let me know, because I can very quickly get that sorted out for you."

By the time Mr. Grit had finished speaking, he had the palms of his hands on the surface of his desk, and was leaned halfway across it, his long, pointed, nose very close to Crook's face.

Crook leaned back in his chair, and then shook his head from side to side, frantically. "No, Sir, no, Sir. That isn't what I meant, Sir. All I meant is that I think I would find a mission like that hard. I didn't mean ours is. I like ours. I made the right choice. I mean, I think I made the right choice."

Mr. Grit, who had just starting lifting himself off his desk, suddenly slammed back down again. "You think you made the right choice?"

Crook felt his heart begin to hammer in his chest, and then shook his head side to side again, even more frantically this time, almost furiously. "No, no, no, Sir. I meant, I know I made the right choice. I know I did..." he trailed off, his voice dropping down to a whisper as if he was now talking to himself rather than Mr. Grit, trying to convince himself. "I know I did, I know I did..."

"Yes, yes, yes!" yelled Mr. Grit. "Good! Great for you! Now enough of your drivel. I told you, I need Plan B implemented, and this is the answer. I need you to make Evergreen drink — I don't care how, I just care when. I need you to do this tomorrow by the latest."

"Tomorrow?" gulped Crook. "Can't I have some time to think about how I can do this?'

"What did I just say?" sneered Mr. Grit. "I said I don't care how you do it, I just want it done — and I just told you when by. We are running out of days, and with everyday that passes us by it's one more day that Father Christmas has on his side; it's one more day that we can't afford. So," he continued, now coming back off his desk and standing back up to his full, tall, narrow self. "You will slip this drink to Evergreen, and then over the course of the day you'll notice his memory begin to fade. He will then be yours for the bending — you'll be able to erase memories, bend facts, tweak truths — anything and everything that you think is necessary to do to ensure that this mission is pulled off. Do I make myself understood?"

"Yes, Sir," replied Crook, immediately.

"Good," said Mr. Grit. He slipped his hand back into the depths of his pocket for a second time, and then pulled out a small, purple pouch, the same shade of purple as the purple glass bottle. He pulled open the drawstrings, loosening the pouch, and then slipped the glass bottle into it. He pulled on the drawstrings, this time tightening then, and then passed the pouch over to Crook.

Mr. Grit then placed Crook's fingers firmly around the pouch, which he had left in the palms of his hands, and then stood back up straight again.

"I'm trusting you on this one, Crook." Mr. Grit said. "You've had your first chance today, and you messed it up. This is your second one, and I mean it when I say that I don't expect you to be wanting — or needing — another chance after this, do you?"

Crook shook his head. "No, Sir."

"Good. Now your hotel room is above mine. Be off to sleep. You've got work to do in the morning."

With that, Mr. Grit dug his hands back into the depths of his coat pockets, and began to sweep out of the room.

"Where are you going, Sir?" Crook asked, turning around in his seat.

Mr. Grit turned back around. "That's," he sneered, "is none of your business. Now good night, Crook."

He stalked away, out of the room, and Crook gulped. "Good night, Sir." then he was left alone in the tall, dark, room, filled with his own nervous thoughts and the illuminations of the moonlight. He gulped again, begin to worry just what it was that he had found himself mixed up with.

But it was too late now. Too late indeed…

24

"WAKE UP!" CAME a voice, blaring through the old warehouse. "Wake up! Wake up!"

The Goblins stirred and murmured, as faint light drifted through the fogged up windows at the top of the warehouse, covered in moss and moulding green ivy, diffusing the light with a hint of greenery.

"'S'morning already?" asked one of the Goblins, his voice cracked and croaky.

"Yes!" exclaimed back Gordon. "Yes it is!"

They rolled onto their backs in their sleeping bags, and began rubbing their eyes, starting to sit up. As they did so, they looked around them, this being the first time they had seen the warehouse in the light of the day, and now that they could see all the details of where they were sleeping, they weren't sure whether or not they would have opted to stay here if they had come here during the daytime.

It was old, musty and damp. The floor was concrete, and in the distance, great, long puddles of water could be seen pooled, stretching into the corners of the warehouse. This didn't help with the issue of the coldness.

When they had first come into the warehouse, they had thought that it was empty, that it had been cleared out when the warehouse had been closed down and put into a state of dis-use, but now, in the light of the day, they could see that, in fact, the old machinery was still there, but now it had been pushed into the corners of the warehouse, and lined up against the walls. They were all brown and yellow and rusted, great big masses of iron and steel, tubes, pipes and pistons. None of the Goblins, no matter how much they looked at them, could quite make out what the machinery were or what it was that they had been used for, their purposes individually, but also collectively, unfathomable.

"Are we all awake?" Gordon said, his voice echoing around the warehouse and ricocheting off the walls.

A murmur of a dozen goblins came back to him, signaling that the answer was yes.

"Good," Gordon replied, pleasing. He grabbed his backpack and began to dig around in it.

"We're hungry," said one of the Goblins.

"Us, too," came a voice from one of the sacks. The Goblins were taken by surprise for a moment, and then remembered what they had done the night before — remembered that they had committed a crime, kidnapped some of the Elves and the Goblins, and that they were still within the darkness of the scratchy sacks.

"Yes, yes, yes," Gordon grumbled, shooshing them and raising his hands in the air, flapping them up and down to get them all to be quiet. "What do you think I'm doing?"

They watched as out of his backpack he withdrew two bundles of bananas, and then began snapping them off.

“A banana?” asked one of the Goblins.

“Yes, Felix — a banana. What did you expect? A banquet? There’s only so much room I have in my backpack — I didn’t see anybody else think about food, did I? If I didn’t think about it, if I hadn’t have been willing to carry it, do you think any of us would be eating at all this morning?”

He was met with a silence.

“Just as I thought,” he grumbled. “Just as I thought!”

With that he began calling out the names of the Goblins and tossing them all a banana each through the air. The Goblins grumbled, but caught the pieces of fruit as they flew through the air.

Then Gordon turned around to face those that they had kidnapped, who were in their sacks in a different cluster to the Goblins, and threw them all bananas.

“How come they get the same as us?” complained one of the Goblins.

“Because bananas are all that we’ve got,” answered Gordon.

“Then surely we should get two each and they should get one each?”

Gordon rolled his eyes. “Will you all stop complaining and just eat up? Just be thankful you’ve got something to eat at all, will you?”

The Goblins looked between one another, sidewards glancing so that Gordon wouldn’t notice, and then returned to their pieces of fruit. In front of them, Gordon bit the end of his banana off, and then began to munch, one arm crossing the front of his body, obviously in a sulk.

The Elves who had been kidnapped looked between one another, too, side-eying each other as they ate their own bananas. They couldn't believe what they were seeing in front of their eyes, couldn't believe the way the Goblins were acting — it was a miracle they had all managed to band together and pull off a kidnapping, and if the kidnapped Elves had been — well, hadn't have been kidnapped — then they thought they would have been laughing at the way the Goblins were acting.

Once everybody had polished their bananas off, Gordon made Felix walk around and collect the banana skins from the rest of the Goblins and the Elves in one of the dis-used potato sacks, and stood up to speak.

"Now then, now that we're all fed, it's time for the day to begin, and time to get down to business." Everybody listened carefully, shuffling up and finishing the murmurings of their private conversations in hushed tones. "As I said last night, I want this mission to be pulled off smoothly and successfully, but the only way we're going to be able to achieve that is if we co-operate both effectively and efficiently. Do I make myself understood?"

Everybody nodded.

"I want you lot to form an orderly queue — and a quiet one at that — in single-file, in front of myself," He gestured to the kidnapped bunch, "and I've got the microphone and transmitter devices here," As he spoke he gestured to a small pouch that he had displayed the night before, "and I'm going to attach them to the Elves. Then we're going to release them, where they must then go home and go into hiding, whilst we take over their identities. As I have said, we have transmitter devices attached to them, not just the microphones, so if any of them do not do what they're told, then they'll be in trouble. Again, do I make myself understood?"

This time, he was talking to the kidnapped Elves. They all nodded back in response.

"Good," Gordon said, evidently pleased. "Now, you lot," he continued, this time speaking back to his team of Goblins, "are also going to have microphone and transmitter devices attached to you. Like I said last night, this will ensure that The Northerly Herald can receive all the information they require to be able to write well-informed reports and articles for publication that will be of the upmost accuracy and high-quality, and so it is important and vital that none of you tamper with them, or remove them from your clothing. We, like we will with the associates," he used this word to distance himself from the crime they all knew they had committed, but everybody knew he meant those who they had kidnapped, "will be able to know where you are at any time, so if you any of you make any attempt to disrupt this mission, then there will be consequences — and, believe it when I tell you, I wouldn't want to be on the receiving end of any consequences that Ms. Edwina Inksmith would want to enforce, myself included. For the last time, do I make myself understood?"

This time it was the Goblin's turn to nod. They all did.

"Good," Gordon said once more. "So, what are we all waiting

for? Get moving everyone!"

The room became a sudden flutter of movement as everyone registered what Gordon had said. They had a plan, and they had to follow it.

Gordon had to admit he felt nervous - it all seemed like such a big operation, but he knew the moment they managed to break into the HQ and pass their disguises off, then he would be happy, because — he hoped — it would all get easier from there on in.

The thought of it all, secretly, made his heart hammer. But the others couldn't know that…

25

NIGHT-TIME HAD fallen over the North Pole.

It was another harsh night. The snow had started to fall mid-afternoon, and the conditions had gotten drastically worse as the sun had sunk lower overhead, before slipping behind the horizon and blanketing the world into darkness. Nobody had seen the sky all day, but rather thick snow clouds that had quickly developed and swarmed over the Town.

As darkness had taken over, the biting coldness had come with it, too, and the snow turned to sleet, feeling like harsh bullets when they bite into your skin when they hit you. The wind was picking up too, turning into an almighty gust, nipping at you and trying its best to freezing through your skin and bite into your bones, sinking you with a terrible coldness into your very insides.

The villagers pulled closed their window-shutters, trying their best to do everything in their power to not let the cold creep into their homes. They lit huge fires in their fireplaces, crackling and roaring in their homes. The air above the North Pole Town filled with smoke that was quickly carried away with the blustery conditions. Everybody was told to stay indoors, and on the television news a storm was announced — everybody was advised to not leave their homes throughout the night, and if anybody was out now then to go immediately to the home of their closest friend or relative to make sure they were kept out of the conditions, so that they came to no harm — but nobody was out anyway. In storms like this, up in the North Pole, nobody can go out — except for Father Christmas and his reindeers, but they were magically equipped to deal with situations like this one, but that was only if the weather turned like this on Christmas Eve.

Tonight, however, was not Christmas Eve, but rather an ordinary night — or, at least, so everybody thought.

As the Town settled into their homes for the night, hoping that the storm would pass them by, allowing it to rage on into the night and hoping that by the time they all awoke in the morning, that calmness would have been restored and settled over the town, nobody had quite expected for their radio stations, the television programmes, that they were watching to be interrupted by an apology and an announcement of some breaking news that everybody needed to know. Everybody in the Town heard the same words of the same broadcast:

"This is breaking news that we have heard directly from the North Pole Headquarters, sources close to Father Christmas have confirmed. It is being reported that Father Christmas has agreed to go to the Court of the Naughty and the Nice, as investigations continue to discover just what happened when young elf, Mr. Evergreen, fell from the top of the Christmas Tree in the North Pole Town Square on December the First, sustaining an injury to his head.

"Furthermore, although it has been reported that Mr. Evergreen has returned to the HQ to work, the cause behind his fall has yet to be confirmed. Some rumours have been going around suggesting it was a problem with the ladder — the very ladder that is supposed to be bewitched to ensure that nobody can fall off it is to blame, thus putting the responsibility of this incident with the Logistics Department. Some have blamed the fact that this year the tree was the tallest tree that they have had in history, which puts the blame with the Head Team, as it is reported that Mr. Christmas' Deputy, Mr. Frederick Jingelton, is the person who chooses the tree — which, this year, was not a natural tree and had magic cast over it to grow it to the size that it was, which has — as we have observed — posed risks to the community and has greatly impacted Mr. Evergreen's December.

"However, others have rumoured that this was nothing to do with Mr. Christmas or anybody else within the HQ Team, but rather the blame is to be pinpointed on somebody who is acting from within the North Pole. As discussed during this broadcast and in the media in recent times, this has never happened before, and so whether it could be a evil force trying to intercept with the Christmas planning within the North Pole is to be debated — the problem with this theory, however, is that if Mr. Christmas says this is true, thus taking any blame and responsibility off of him and his Team, although suggesting his Security Team may not be up to scratch in their standards and thoroughness, is that it will then panic the public. Alternatively, if Mr. Christmas wishes to deny this theory, then the blame must lie with himself and his Teams and his Departments.

"So, Mr. Christmas will be taken to the Court of the Naughty and the Nice, and hopefully the root of all of this can be discovered, and the public will finally be given the answers that we all so much deserve. This is Barbara McCurrant, Northerly Live. Thank you."

The broadcast suddenly went fuzzy on the screens and the radios, and then vanished, leaving in its wake either silence, or the television programme or music the watchers and the listeners had on before the emergency broadcast interrupted their nights. Everybody in their homes looked to one another; they were all shocked over what they had heard. Nobody could believe it — in all their time they had been alive, even the older generations, it had never been heard that a Father Christmas was to be presented to the Court of the Naughty and the Nice, as though he had committed some sort of a crime.

The children began to panic, starting to ask what would happen if Father Christmas was found to be Naughty, not Nice. Their parents all re-assured them, telling them that Father Christmas hadn't done anything wrong — whatever had happened on that night of December the First had been beyond his control — that the only reason they were taking this whole matter, this whole situation, to the Court was so they could find out the answers that everybody wanted to know.

But, secretly, some parents and grandparents weren't too sure what they thought, weren't too sure what they believed or what they should believe. Nothing like this had ever happened before, and they could feel that the Town would be split over this — the more that time went on, the more that different people would start thinking, start believing, different things.

Right now, as soon as the broadcast had finished, everybody wanted to go out, wanted to hear what different people thought to what they had all seen, what they had all heard, but the weather was too terrible and they had been advised to stay indoors.

With the storm raging on, the news that had spread begun to sink in, and the Town, without even seeing one another, without even speaking to one another, began to divide.

Up in his hotel room, Mr. Grit twiddled his fingertips and cackled. This plan was turning out to be working better and better, and more and more in his favour, than he had even planned it to do so.

Down in his living room, Father Christmas sunk his face into the palms of his hand and exhaled. This was all turning out to be a mess and even he himself didn't know what to believe.

In the middle of town, Evergreen heard the news and felt guilty, as though he was somehow to blame, but he was as clueless as ever.

Nobody knew what was going to happen next; nobody knew how this was going to end; nobody had ever seen anything like this before.

26

THE NEXT MORNING Evergreen awoke early, hearing a knocking on his front-door. His bedroom was still in half-darkness, and even though it was wintertime in the North Pole, he never normally woke up for work when it was still dark outside.

Sliding out of bed and rubbing his eyes, he slipped on his slippers and wandered out his bedroom door, padded down the stairs, and through his house to his front door.

He pulled it open, not sure of what or who to expect.

"Hell—"

"Good morning, good morning, to you, and you!" Came a voice, singing back. Evergreen blinked in the darkness, dazed at what was going on.

"Kane?" he said.

"That's right. I thought you would be ready by now!" he exclaimed.

"It's too early!" Evergreen remarked. "I don't usually get ready this early."

"Well, you do now," Kane said, matter-of-factly. "You did say you were thinking about."

"I did? When?"

"Just before you had your fall!" Kane shot back, as though this was obvious, common knowledge.

"Oh. I… I can't remember saying that."

Kane shrugged his shoulders. "Well, whether you can or whether you can't, it doesn't really matter now, does it?"

Evergreen was still confused, but then he shrugged his own shoulders. "Well, I guess… I guess no, I suppose it doesn't." He blinked several more times, as though some sort of a cloud had suddenly fogged up his mind, which — in a way — is exactly what was happening. The lie that Kane had made up was colliding with Evergreen's real memories, because of course Evergreen had not once said he wanted to go into work earlier, not once expressed a wish to be in work before anyone else had arrived. As far as he was concerned, he was quite happy doing what he had always done, and that was how he always planned to continue - not once had he ever wanted that to change.

Or, at least, until now — because as Evergreen spoke, his memories began to change, and a new memory started to form, slowly, slowly erasing out the real, legitimate one. "I think… I think I do remember that now," he said, slowly at first but quickening his pace as the false memory came to him. "I suppose I better go and start getting ready then, hadn't I?"

"I think so," smiled Kane. "I think so."

Evergreen smiled, and then said, "Would you like to come in whilst I get ready? I don't think I'll be long."

Kane nodded. "Thank you," and then stepped over the threshold as Evergreen shut the door behind them. Because he had stayed there for a night before, he knew where everything was, and he thought he would use this to his advantage. "I'll tell you what," he said, as though he had just had a cracking idea. "Whilst you go upstairs and get ready, I'll make us a drink each, shall I?"

"Ooh," Evergreen said, "I'd appreciate that. A nice hot chocolate or something, hey?"

"Coming up," smiled Kane.

"You know where everything is, don't you?" he asked.

"I do, I do."

"Great!" smiled Evergreen, lighting up as he began to waken. "I'll go upstairs now then."

Kane grinned back encouragingly at Evergreen, watching the young Elf as he turned on the spot and jogged to his stairs, running up them, leaping three steps at a time.

Then, when Evergreen was busy upstairs, safely out of sight, and Kane was safely out of sight of Evergreen, he quickly spun around and made his way to the kitchen, he grabbed the kettle, filled it up with water, and hurriedly set about boiling it. He plucked two mugs out of one of the cupboards, picked up the tub of cocoa powder and spooned in a couple of spoonfuls of it into the bottom of each mug, then got a carton of milk out of the fridge.

Impatiently, he tapped his fingers on the surface of the kitchen worktop, drumming his fingers as he waited for the water in the kettle to finish boiling. The longer he waited, the more impatient he grew, and the longer he seemed to be waiting. He was worried that at any moment now Evergreen would bound back down the stairs and announce that he was ready, and then Kane would have found himself stuck, his mission failed and unsure of what to do, and then he would have had to go back and tell Mr. Grit that he had failed, and that was the last thing he wanted to do, especially as Mr. Grit was beginning to get angsty about the amount of time the mission was taking, and the amount of time that they had left until Christmas Eve.

After what seemed like a lifetime, the kettle finally finished boiling, Kane grabbed it and poured the hot water into the two mugs, steam rising into the air. He picked up a spoon and stirred the cocoa powder in, and then let it settle for a moment, before picking up the milk. He then stirred this in, too, until both hot chocolates were done and ready to go.

He picked his up and set it on the side, and then he turned back to the other mug of hot chocolate that was left sitting there. He took a step back and took a glance back at the stairs, and when he was sure that Evergreen was still upstairs and getting ready, he stepped back up to the mug, slipped his hands into the interior pocket of his jacket, and pulled out the small, purple bottle made out of glass that Mr. Grit had given him the night before.

Raising the glass in the air, he tipped it from side to side, watching the liquid slowly ooze from one side to the other. A thin smile crossed his face, thinking about just how powerful this small purple bottle was, the possibilities that were withheld within it, and then he screwed the silver lid off the top. He turned the bottle upside down, and then began to pour the liquid into the hot chocolate. The liquid was more like honey than water, and it seemed to take an eternity to empty. All the time as he was pouring, Kane was stirring the mixture, which reminded him more of a cough medicine than a magical sort of potion, with a spoon, trying to blend it into the hot drink.

As the final few drops oozed into the drink, he flicked the bottle and tapped it on the bottom, making sure he could get every bit of it out, and then screwed the lid back onto the top of it, then slipped the bottle back into his jacket pocket. He stirred the last bits of it into the hot chocolate, then crossed over to the sink, washed the spoon in water from the tap so that nothing suspicious could be found, then grabbed the hot chocolate and set it on the side for Evergreen, who — just at that very moment — bounded back down the stairs.

Kane heard him coming, and sighed a quiet sigh of relief that he had managed to do it all in time, and grabbed his own hot chocolate, raising it to his mouth and taking a sip just as Evergreen walked into the room.

"There's yours," Kane said, gesturing to the mug on the top of the breakfast bar, after swallowing his own mouthful. "I hope you like it. I think I've done a good job."

"Aw, thank you ever so much," Evergreen said, picking up the mug. He raised it to his mouth and took a big gulp of it, and for a moment Kane watched him over the top of his own mug, hoping, praying, that it would taste okay, that Evergreen wouldn't say anything, that he wouldn't suspect anything.

After a moment which seemed to stretch onto in forever, Evergreen brought the mug back down, hot chocolate around his top lip, and exhaled a satisfied sigh. "That's lovely," he said. "And so sweet, too — just what I need to get me going in the morning."

Kane didn't say anything, but just smiled back instead. Inside, Kane, the real identity being Bing and not even Crook, felt his stomach turn to lead for a split second. He was unsure of whether he was doing the right thing, whether he was doing something that even he thought was going too far, wondered whether he should feel like a criminal committing some sort of unforgivable crime, but then he remembered what Mr. Grit had said, and he remembered how he had felt when he had been living in the North Pole, when he had been working at the HQ, and the moment suddenly ended. He had to do this, he told himself. He had no choice, he reminded himself. This was for the better, he pressed into himself. He swiped the other thoughts of his own mind, and got himself to snap back into how he should be thinking, re-focusing on the mission he had in hand that he needed to do, that he needed to complete.

Evergreen glanced at the watch on his wrist. "I think we better get a move on, don't you?"

Then with that he gulped down the rest of hot chocolate, let out another sigh with a smack of his lips, and slapped the empty mug back down onto the top of the breakfast bar.

Kane gulped, then nodded. He drank a few more mouthfuls of the rest of his own hot chocolate, then decided he didn't want anymore, and tossed the rest down the sink.

Turning back around, he pulled his jacket tighter around his body as Evergreen was slipping on his coat.

"Ready to go?" he asked.

"Ready as ever," grinned Evergreen.

Kane felt his stomach weigh him down just a tiny bit more.

There was nothing he could do now though — Evergreen had already drunk the contents of the purple bottle.

It was too late.

27

EVERGREEN CLOSED HIS front door behind him with a thud, and then span around on the doorstep, flashing Kane a great big smile.

"It's a lovely day, isn't it?" he asked, looking between Kane and the sky.

Following Evergreen's glances, Kane looked up to the sky. Evergreen was right. The storm that had happened the night before had gone; there was no sign it had ever even happened. It was as though they had all just dreamed it. There were no trees that had fallen on the road, no sign-posts that had been knocked over, nothing on any of the houses that had been broken. It was all rather bizarre, and even more so now the sun was shining and the sky was clear blue.

"I love Christmas," Evergreen said, as they made their way down his garden path towards his gate, "and I love wintertime, too, now don't get me wrong, but," he continued, pleasantly chatty, "I love Spring. The feel of the warmth of the sun on your skin, the scent of the flowers tickling your nose, the sound of fizzing lemonade and ice-cubes chinking against the cold glass. Do you know what I mean?" he asked.

Kane just stared at the back of his head as they walked, stepping onto the main road and making their way to the HQ. "Not really," he said, plainly.

"What do you mean, "not really"?" Evergreen exclaimed. "You mean to say you don't like Spring?"

"That would be correct."

"How about Summer?"

"Definitely not."

"I do."

"You're supposed to be an Elf!"

"I am an Elf. Doesn't mean I can't enjoy hot weather."

Kane grumbled.

"Autumn then?"

"A little better."

"Winter."

"Is my favourite," finished Kane.

"But why? Everything is so cold and so miserable and so damp!" Evergreen said, as though he was in a pantomime and being over-dramatic over the way he was speaking.

Kane shrugged his shoulders, squinting in the low morning sunlight. "I don't know," he said. "It just is. Now stop asking me questions — the sun might be out but it's still too cold to dawdle along chatting."

Evergreen was quite taken aback, but he did as he was told. Kane, meanwhile, continued walking straight ahead, towards the HQ, he tried to maintain his thoughts on what the day ahead held. But, as he walked, he couldn't help but think about the questions Evergreen had asked him. Truthfully, Kane had liked all the seasons, once upon a time, and he had loved summer just as much as he had loved the winter — but summer just held bad memories for him.

In the North Pole, Summer is the time of vacation. They're still busy, still producing toys and making plans, just as they do all year round, but in the Summer times get a little more lenient. Nights where they could just spend it sipping fizzy drinks sat outside in a garden; mornings where they could just amble along to work; months where sometimes they were given the whole of a week off work, where they didn't need to go into the HQ at all.

He had never understood it.

He had never understood why just because the sun was shining meant they had to miss time off work. He was never into playing games, and he was never very good at them, either. Which was, probably, now that he looked back on it, why he never liked playing games in the first instance. His twin brother was always the better one at games — he was also the best at kicking a ball, the winner at running races, the champion when it came to making homemade lemonade — he'd always sell more, make more, chat more. Just like the cold months where Kane felt as though Bong would overshadow everything he did, the warmer months became just the same.

As he had gotten older, up until he had chosen to try to push for himself to be Banished, Crook had become to love the winter instead — he loved the darkness, he loved the shadows, he loved how it became deemed okay to spend more time by yourself, pouring over books or planning things. And now, as a full-time villain, winter meant that he got to do all of those fun things, and all the more often.

His thoughts were sent scattering away as they reached the HQ entrance. The Security Guard, the plump Goblin, was sat snoozing in his box. Evergreen went to knock on the side of it, waking him up rudely from his slumber, but Kane quickly leaned forward and snapped his hands around Evergreen's thin wrist.

"No, no, no," he cried, under a whisper. "Just leave him to sleep."

"Well, we need to be checked!"

Kane rolled his eyes. "Have you got anything dangerous on you?"

Evergreen shook his head.

"There you go then."

"That's not the point," Evergreen sulked. "It's the principle."

"Principle, schwimciple."

But the two of them must have been louder than they'd realised, because the Security Goblin yawned and then looked at them both.

"Just us again!" smiled Kane, standing up straight all of a sudden, letting go of his hold on Evergreen's wrist, so his arm went suddenly thumping back against his side.

"Ow!" Evergreen exclaimed. Kane elbowed him discreetly in his side. The Security Guard frowned, but was too sleepy for it to register.

"Go in, go in…" he said. "Recognise you from yesterday…" And then, just like that, he dropped off again.

Kane had to cover up a big smirk. It was honestly as though the HQ were trying to help him succeed in messing up their plans without them even knowing about it.

"Come on, then," Kane grumbled, his smile suddenly vanishing now the Guard was back asleep again. "We haven't got all day."

Evergreen watched as Kane began to march forward, shook his head and rolled his eyes, then made off after him, puzzled as to how someone could change their mood so quickly.

But, as he did follow Kane, he couldn't help but think about how it was as though there was more going on than what met the eye, and right under his nose too, but then it was as if as soon as this thought entered his head something came along in his mind and sucked it up and threw it out, and made him forget all about it.

And, sure enough, a split second after thinking this thought, Evergreen suddenly found himself stood there, confused, trying to remember what it was he had been stood thinking about.

"I said come on!" Kane called from up ahead.

Evergreen realised he'd stop walking, shook his head firmly and told himself what for, and then got going again, unsure of why he had ever stopped in the first place.

28

ON THE SAME morning as Evergreen and Kane walked into one side of the HQ, the Goblins were walking out of the other side, feeling triumphant of what they had managed to achieve.

Sneaking into the HQ had been easier than they had expected — they couldn't believe that the simple matter of wearing a few disguises had helped them to succeed in passing Security. Gordon said it must have been to do with the fact there were so many of them.

"I just don't think any of us could have gotten through alone," he said. "I think we'd have been too obvious, but there was no way they could suspect a dozen people of being in disguise, especially when we're wearing the same uniforms."

The others had all nodded in agreement, but whilst they were all delighted at their success of the day of pretending to be regular, working elves, and their success of the night of causing mischief, they all had someone else playing on their minds: Edwina Inksmith, for Edwina was the real one they had to impress.

All the time, they had been scribbling down notes in every few moments they got, so when nobody else had been looking they had been able to document exactly what they had seen and what had gone on. As the night had drawn to a close, Gordon had collated everyone's notes into a big stack, and was now ruffling through them as they made their way back to the warehouse for some rest.

"Have I got everyone's notes?" he asked.

They all murmured, most of inaudible, but Gordon took that as a yes.

"Good," he said. "Now, I want you all back to the warehouse, make sure you all get some rest — we've got a lot more work ahead of us if we want to be able to do this all right — and I'm going to go back to the Herald and hand Edwina these notes. If we're quick enough, we might be able to get in quick enough for the lunchtime issue."

The Goblins grinned to each other at this thought, a couple of them rubbing their hands together, but the majority of them just rubbed their eyes instead. They were tired, not used to staying up all night, and all they wanted was a few hours of kip.

As they finally reached the warehouse. Gordon bade them all goodbye, and then took off at a run, back towards The Northerly Herald as the Goblins piled about in their sleeping backs, and went back to sleep.

* * *

As Father Christmas woke up, he was increasingly aware of how many days there were left now until Christmas Eve, and just how much he had to do. He was beginning to feel stressed, but — at the same time

— he was beginning to feel excited. It was always around this time of the month when he began to realise that, for another year running, they were going to be able to pull it off, and make millions, in fact billions, of people happy all around the world. He was never quite sure just how they managed to do it, but he knew they always did, and he was fairly certain that this year wouldn't be any different, regardless of what the newspapers were saying, or whatever people were thinking — he was going to prove them wrong, and show them all that he can still do Christmas, that he is still able to make it magical, that he should be the man — the best man — to the job — the best job in the world, if he said so himself.

With this, he slid out of bed and went about getting himself ready. He trimmed his beard and brushed his long hair, got dressed in his red suit and pulled on his big, black boots. Looking in the mirror in his and Mrs. Claus' small bedroom, he gave himself a smile and a wink, and then went down stairs.

"Morning, dear," he called aloud, as he reached the bottom, the living room coming into sight. It was warm and cosy, a huge fire crackling in the open hearth.

"Morning, love," Mrs. Claus called back. "You'll have to make your own breakfast. I'm too busy."

Father Christmas nodded, seeing that Mrs. Claus was surrounded by papers and letters, addresses and stamps. One of her many responsibilities, for Mrs. Claus worked very heavily within the Christmas business, was making sure that every child's letter that comes in to the North Pole is noticed and recognised and attempted to be followed by as closely as possible, and making sure that every child who has asked for a letter from the North Pole gets one sent out! And it was always at this time of the month when they got another surge of letters, after the steady stream had died off, because people realise just how soon Christmas is, how quickly it's come around once more, and hurriedly send a letter to the North Pole before they run out of time — meaning Mrs. Claus didn't have much time for any leeway on these letters. They needed sorted and replying to, and they needed doing quickly.

"No problem," Father Christmas said, and he took himself through to the kitchen, where he grabbed himself a bottle of milk and two cookies. "I'm going to get off to the office myself now, anyway. Lot's to do today — we've got the List inspection just before lunch.

Mrs. Claus nodded, but didn't look up, too busy sorting through her letters. "Right you are then," she called back. Then: "What have you got yourself for breakfast?"

"Just some fruit."

He was met with a laugh. "Yeah, right. I don't think in all the years we've been together you've ever gotten yourself fruit if you get to choose what to have for your breakfast. What have you really got?"

"Fruit," Father Christmas insisted.

"Cookies, you mean."

"Maybe."

"And milk."

"Okay, okay," chuckled Father Christmas. "You caught me out, but I just can't resist."

"It's a good job I'm busy," replied Mrs. Claus. "Now be off with you. I've got work to do and you don't want to be late."

Father Christmas nodded back, turned around with his boots making a big, squeaky sound against the wooden floorboards, and then stepped out the door. He walked through a small garden, then opened up another door that was built into the side of a huge, brick wall, and then stepped through it. He was inside the HQ. Being the top man, he needed to be able to access the HQ at any time, and so his house was the closest house in all the North Pole in relation to the HQ — and it was also the most guarded, too, Security Goblins constantly all the way around it.

"Morning, Bert."

"Morning, Sir," smiled a Goblin as Santa appeared through the door, the cold air rushing in behind him. Bert was the Security Goblin who Guarded this door during the day.

"How's things looking today?" Father Christmas asked, stopping to talk for a moment.

"Things are looking calm at the moment, Sir. Everything's running smoothly."

"Good, good," mumbled Father Christmas, more to himself than back to Bert. "Keep up the great work, won't you?"

Bert nodded back, grinning back at Father Christmas who gave him a small wink, and then he made his way off again, venturing into the HQ and towards his office, feeling good about the day ahead.

* * *

Back on the other side of the HQ, Evergreen and Kane were getting ready to start their day of work. Evergreen had still found Kane's behaviour odd, but having forgotten what exactly about Kane he had found odd, he decided it must be him who was being the odd one, and pushed the thoughts out of his head.

Pulling on his gloves and getting ready to inspect some of the newly-made toys, Evergreen was eager to get started. He sat down at his stool at his workbench, Kane next to him, and picked up the first toy, when all of a sudden something sharp jabbed him in the ribs.

"Ouch!" he exclaimed, rather loudly, too loudly than he had meant to.

A few of the other Elves who were working around him peered over from their desks and workbenches, inquisitive as to who had made the noise and why.

"Keep it down!" Kane said, urgently, under is breath.

"Everything okay, Evergreen?" came a voice.

Evergreen leaned back on his stool and looked over. "Yes thank, Pintruckle. Just pricked myself with a pin on this toy part, that's all okay."

Pintruckle nodded, satisfied with the answer, and then shuffled out, back to her own work. She had been working at the HQ for many years, probably since Evergreen's parent's generation, she was an old Elf, but very wise. She was very good at picking up on any problem, and usually nothing slipped by her notice if she had anything to do with it.

"What was that for?" Evergreen whispered, turning back around once he was sure nobody else was watching, turning to face Kane. "That hurt."

"Oh, well I am sorry," moaned Kane, being sarcastic. "It was meant to get your attention."

"Well I do have a name, you know."

"Yeah, I know you do," replied Kane.

"Well, use it then," retorted Evergreen.

Kane shook his head from side to side. "Enough, enough. Enough already. We need to do something."

Evergreen frowned. "And what's that then?"

And this is the point where Kane suddenly found himself extremely nervous, because this is the part where everything could go wrong, where the whole plan could collapse and Kane would find himself and Mr. Grit in big trouble. It all depended on just how well the purple memory liquid in the little glass bottle had worked on Evergreen. If it had worked well enough, then this next part of the plan would work smoothly, with no problems at all. If not, if the liquid hadn't worked, if Evergreen's memory hadn't been modified, then Evergreen might confess to everyone else what Kane was about to say, and out him, and thus outing Mr. Grit, putting an end to their plan, and

— most likely — putting an end to the newly-found career of being a villain that Kane was getting used to. As much as sometimes he had found himself wondering whether he should be regretting his change in career, whenever he thought about it being taken away from him, he very quickly decided that being a villain was actually exactly what he liked doing, and working back here, back at the HQ, all the time, for the rest of time, was the last thing that he wanted to be doing with his life.

He shuddered at the thought, and then it was this that helped to spur him on. "We need to do something together, but it's quite risky, and so I must ask you to not tell anybody else what we're doing."

"Is it something that's going to get the pair of us into trouble?" Evergreen asked. "Because if it is, then I'm afraid I want to have no part to play in it."

"No, no, no," Kane said, spinning round on his stool so that he could fully face Evergreen. "It's nothing at all that will get us into trouble — it's something we're supposed to do, something we've been asked to do."

"What? The two of us?" he asked, curiously.

"Yeah," smiled Kane, trying to look comforting, reassuring, making everything seem bigger than it was. "It\s a huge responsibility, and that's why it's risky, and that's why it's important that you keep your voice down — we don't want anybody else to get jealous, but we also don't want anybody else to know what we're doing, in case they decide to intercept."

"Intercept what?" Evergreen pressed, growing impatient with Kane. He just wanted to know what he was talking about, and he wanted to know now.

"We need to get the key that goes to the Naughty or Nice List Department."

Evergreen nearly choked on his own gasp. "But nobody can go in there."

Kane chewed the inside of his mouth. Evergreen wasn't supposed to be able to remember these small details. "We can," he said, starting slow, trying to convince Evergreen, trying not to startle him, "if we've been asked to do it. If we're the one's who has been given permission from Mr. Christmas to do so."

"And what do we need to do whilst we're in there?" he asked.

"Oh," Kane said, casually, as though this was just something he did everyday. "I just need to change a few names over on the list. Father Christmas mentioned that some people who were Nice have now been Naughty, and that some people who have been Naughty have been Nice."

"Why can't he change them over himself?" Evergreen pondered.

"Because he's running this place! He's a busy man, Evergreen — you can't expect him to do everything round here, can you?" Kane retorted.

"I know, I know. I was just saying."

"Good. Now that's enough of "just saying", though. We've got work to do."

And with that, he hopped off his stool and set off out of the room. He was unsure of where he needed to be going, but sure enough — just as he had predicted — Evergreen jumped off his own stool and scuttled on after him.

Maybe the plan would go to plan after all…

* * *

Father Christmas did just as he had planned.

He went to his office, where he spent a great deal of his morning sorting through letters, finishing off some timetables, proofing some toys, and making sure everything was running just as it should be. He then had a meeting about Christmas Eve, going over it with Goose and Mr. Jingelton, finalising the details and the order of events over the night.

"Sounds good," Father Christmas said, as they reached the end of the list of times and events. "I'll be back just before sunrise, and then I think that will mark our most efficient year yet — which, considering how much the population has grown since last year, and in the last five years too, is something to be proud of."

Goose and Mr. Jingelton nodded, sorting out the paperwork and shuffling their notes. They had been very pleased as to how the meeting had gone themselves.

"Now, if you excuse me," Father Christmas said, "but I'm going to take myself off for my lunch. I'll see you both later, when we go to check the sleigh, yes?" he asked, looking between the two.

They both nodded.

"That you will, Sir," smiled Goose.

"Good good," cheered Father Christmas, patting them both on the back as he made his way around the table, and then wandered out of the room.

As he stepped out of the meeting room, he walked past his office and out of a set of double doors, then into the HQ. His Elves were busy at their desks, and yet more were busy dashing here and hurrying there, back and forth, a confusion of hustle and bustle that looked chaotic to the untrained eye, but an organised and a fine-tuned machine to Father Christmas. He smiled to himself as he made his way through it all, pleased with how the day was going, how everybody was working, how everything seemed to be going to plan, and waved a couple of times to some of the Elves, bowing his head to them and gesturing hello. For the first time since December the First, since Evergreen had fallen off the top of the Christmas tree in the Town Square, Father Christmas could almost feel himself relaxing — relaxing in the sense that he thought the public, the outside world, were beginning to forget about what had happened, despite the fact he had to go to Court, and that by the time it came around that he would have to make his appearance, everybody would see just how well he had done with sorting out Christmas, and they would think, just like he currently did, how crazy it was that he had been summoned to the Court of The Naughty and The Nice in the first place, and perhaps the case would be thrown out and laid to rest, and then he would be allowed to get on with his job as he always did, year after year, with no interruption or any other additional trouble to take up his time.

He left the commotion of the HQ behind him, and walked into his private quarters, coming to a stop in his kitchen and sitting down at the kitchen table. His lunch was also made and prepared for him — he had turkey sandwiches with cranberry sauce, and some carrot sticks on the side with a small selection of dips. Not a mince pie was in sight — it made him a bit sad. He supposed the kitchen staff were already putting him on a diet, despite the fact the Christmas season had barely gotten underway yet. He could have sworn his diet that he was put on every year seemed to start earlier and earlier with every year that came along. Soon, he was sure of it, they'd have him on a diet seven days a week, twelve months a year — basically, all the blooming time. He was certain he wasn't going to let them get away with it.

With thoughts of his diet clouding his head, Father Christmas was shocked when Mrs. Christmas came dashing into the kitchen, a newspaper in her hand and a startled expression covering her face.

"What ever is the matter with you?" Father Christmas asked, for it was almost as if she had seen a ghost.

"It's this," she said, holding the copy of the newspaper in her hand. "There's a new report in the paper — but it most certainly can't be true. Can it?"

Father Christmas shook his head. "I don't know," he said. "I can't know if I haven't read it yet, can I?"

Mrs. Christmas reached the table and tossed the newspaper in front of Father Christmas. He went to look down at it, but then — at that exact moment –– the kitchen doors flew open once more, and in came Mr. Jingelton and Goose, the pair of them in just as much of an urgent hurry as Mrs. Christmas had been. Both of them, too, had a copy of the newspaper in their hands.

"Have you seen it, Sir?" Goose asked.

"It can't be true," Mr. Jingelton said.

"We'll have to check," Mrs. Christmas added.

"But how can they know before us?" Goose wondered.

"We must have spies!" Mr. Jingelton worried aloud.

"But how?" Goose said.

"And why?" Mrs. Christmas said, anxiously.

"Now, now, now!" Father Christmas said, raising his voice all of a sudden. "How am I expected to read when I can barely get a moment of silence? You've all come in here worrying and packing and hurtling about like a bunch of headless chickens! Hush a moment and let me read so I can know what's going on. Honestly, sometimes it feels as though it's forgotten that it's supposed to be me who runs this place."

The three of them looked from one to the other, nervously, as Father Christmas looked them all over, shook his head, and then pushed his half-moon spectacles further up his nose so that he was able to get a good look at the newspaper, which he brought up closer to his face, and then he began to read:

SANTA WORRIED AS SLEIGH BROKEN

It has emerged from sources that the sleigh which Father Christmas uses every year to make his annual trip around the world on Christmas Eve, the twenty-fourth of December, is reportedly broken. It looks as though vandals have had something to do with it, although further sources add that "no break has happened", and that "no break in could have happened".

This, of course, raises further concerns — does this mean that the sleigh has just been left unattended or maintained all year long? If no break in has happened, perhaps the attention that a vehicle and machine as special and as unique as the sleigh has just been left to fall to bits over the last twelves months. As even a normal car would do so, if left alone and not looked after over a long period of time, natural damage takes place.

However, what is most suspicious about this is that Father Christmas and his Head Team at the HeadQuarters have made no comment about this incident, nor have they made any report about the condition of the sleigh. Sources have also confirmed that none of the Head Team, including Father Christmas himself, have booked in any appointments in order to be able to have the sleigh repaired, and with time ticking, it begins to lead to further questioning as to just how good Father Christmas is at running operations within the HeadQuarters.

It has been noted that it should have been this afternoon that Father Christmas and his Team were to be expected to perform checks on the sleigh, but some may conspire that this is merely a

fake truth — one that has been hastily made-up to act as though the Head Team and Mr. Christmas are on top of events at the North Pole.

For Mr. Christmas himself, this could not have come at a worse time — in just a few days he is expected to make his first of a series of appearances at the Court of The Naughty and The Nice, after being summoned by the Courts in order to be able to get to the bottom of just what happened on the night of December the First, when young Evergreen the Elf toppled from the top of the Christmas Tree in the North Pole Town Square, after being elected by the Committee to place the star upon the tree, after being named the Star Elf, the Elf of the Year. He was subsequently injured and subject to time off work, and no answers were given, leading to speculation that either outside forces contributed to this disaster and thus we have problems with the Security Team, or that something went wrong with the tree.

So far, the public have been left clueless, and — now, as it stands — we've now got something else to be concerned about, too.

Just what is Father Christmas doing in the North Pole, and why is performance beginning to slack?

As the events unfold, and as things tend to come in threes, we can't help but ask ourselves: just what is going to happen next?

Edwina Inksmith, The Northerly Herald

Father Christmas dropped the newspaper down onto the top of the table, and then looked up at the other three.

"Exactly," they all said, at the same time, noticing his face growing paler and paler with every second that passed them by.

"I don't understand," he said. "I… I…" he continued to stammer. "It doesn't make sense. I don't get it."

"Neither do we, Sir," Goose said. "On my way here to see you I contacted the Head of the Security Team to try and see if anything funny had gone on in the last couple of days, but they reported nothing. They said that if anything they've had the lowest number of incidents they've had all year — not one person has tried to break in, or get in, or sneak in, even internally we've had nobody try to get into any of the rooms they shouldn't be in or wander into the wrong areas. If anything, they said it's all been smooth."

"And what about the sleigh?" Father Christmas asked. "Is this article true? Has the sleigh had any damage?"

Mr. Jingelton and Goose looked nervously between one another, unsure of who to talk, when Goose decided to carry on, and took over the answer. "I'm afraid I can't answer you on that one, Sir. Nobody has checked."

Father Christmas looked stern. "Well, why not? An article like this one is printed and nobody bothers to check?"

"With all due respect, Sir," Goose said, "we thought it more important to come here first and let you know what's gone on, and that way we can keep you in the loop and ask what you think is the best thing to do. Plus — again, with all due respect, Sir — I thought it was scheduled for us all to go and perform checks on the sleigh just this afternoon. I didn't think any of us would have to go early if we were all going along this afternoon."

Father Christmas stayed still for a moment, but then his shoulders sagged a little, and he appeared to soften. He knew Goose was right. "That's very true," he said. "I apologise."

"I understand, Sir. An apology isn't needed."

"Well, still," Father Christmas said. "I'd like to give you one. I'd like to give you all one — I know you're all just as baffled by this as I am, and I shouldn't take it out on you. We're in this together, and we're going to make sure we get to the bottom of this — and we're going to need to do so pretty quickly. A lot of people are going to be asking a lot of questions right now, and we need to be able to give them a lot of answers. Am I understood?"

They all nodded.

"Good," he said back. "Now then, let's not waste another moment — we need to get down to the sleigh room."

He stood back up and slipped his jacket back on, and with that he marched out of the room, throwing his sandwich back down. The others tossed their copies of their newspapers on top of Father Christmas', and then made off after him in a hurry.

As they left the room, the sandwiches on Father Christmas' plate were barely touched, and they would be forgotten about for the rest of the day. If anything, Father Christmas supposed, at least his diet was going a little bit better than planned, since he just wasn't being given the time to eat.

It was all getting rather stressful, and it was all getting very confusing.

Edwina Inksmith was very pleased with herself, and very pleased with her Goblins, which they were very pleased to hear about.

29

MR. GRIT FINISHED reading the newspaper report, and then put it aside himself, and then he stood up and began to pace his hotel room, back and forth, back and forth, just as he always did when he was deep in thought.

It was interesting, he thought, that The Northerly Herald kept publishing these reports against the North Pole, against Father Christmas. It was almost as though they purposefully wanted to make him look bad, rather than just report what was going on. Mr. Grit knew the rest of the public would just believe it, but Mr. Grit, although not a journalist, knew how bad things worked, and he knew the signs of bad things, how to spot them, how to read them, how to know when there was more going on behind closed doors than what was meeting the eye.

After a lot of thought, he turned around the balls of his feet, and slipped on his cape, his long, long black coat, and his black hat, black gloves, and grabbed his black briefcase, and left the hotel room. It was freezing cold, the hotel room, just as Mr. Grit liked it. The tall window was open, the silk curtain blowing and curling into the air, white against the darkness of the night, looking like some hovering ghost, the moonlight shining through it and casting dancing shadows on the floor, and so the coldness outside didn't come as a shock to Mr. Grit.

He stalked his way through the night, walking through the snow with precision and carefulness, his thin figure perfect for walking over ice. He didn't weigh too much, and so he didn't have very much potential to slip. He went over the hills and around the edge of town, as the moon continued to creep higher into the sky as the night drew on.

It wasn't until he reached a building on the edge of town that he came to a stop. Huge letters above the doorway, printed in the same font a newspaper would use, read THE NORTHERLY HERALD CO against the old bricks. Mr. Grit grinned to himself, and then walked up through a metal archway and up to a door, and gave a knock, the door fell open.

Shrugging to himself, he walked through and into the building. Unlike the outside, which was very old and made out of brick, the inside was very new, modern and sleek, all glass, white and silver, with green plants in posh vases everywhere. He was starting to think that he might have made some sort of a mistake, that this would be no place for a potential villainess to live and to work. Where was the darkness? Where was the coldness? Where were the shadows?

For a moment, he contemplated leaving, turning around and going back to his abode and returning to his hotel room, when a woman walked out of an office and into sight behind the empty reception, since it was after opening hours.

"Oh," she said, surprised at the sight of a tall, thin man all dressed in black stood in front of her. "I didn't think I had any more appointments today."

"You don't," replied Mr. Grit, his voice low but sharp. "But I just had to see you."

"What about?" she asked.

"What's your name?"

"Edwina," Edwina replied. "Edwina Inksmith." Then: "Why? Who's asking?"

"I am."

"And you are?"

"Mr. Grit," Mr. Grit said back.

She seemed puzzled at his name, for it was a rather peculiar name, but — remaining polite — she accepted it, and the confused expression vanished off her face, so quickly that even Mr. Grit himself doubted whether it was ever really there or not.

"Did you write the article?" he asked.

"Which one?" she pressed. "I write a lot of them. I'm a journalist."

"I know," Mr. Grit smiled back. "And a very good one at that, too."

Edwina Inksmith smiled, too.

"The one about the sleigh, about the failure of the man who's running the HQ."

Edwina Inksmith's smile turned into a smirk. "That was I."

"Well then I need to talk to you."

"About what?" she asked, curiously.

"I've come to strike you a deal — and one I'm pretty sure you won't want to refuse…"

At this, Edwina sat up, placing her elbows on the surface of her desk and resting her chin on her hands, looking up at Mr. Grit. "And just what might that be?"

Mr. Grit stopped pacing up and down, then turned to face Edwina. "I'm not sure whether or not you know, but I, too, have been undergoing an operation to infiltrate the North Pole, to bring it down, and to put a spanner in the works, so to speak."

Edwina was now very interested. "You have?" she asked. "And to think I thought I was the only one doing so." She bit her lip, deep in thought. "What have you been doing then?"

At this, Mr. Grit laughed. "Do you remember that stupid little Elf that fell off the top of the Christmas Tree on December the First?"

"You mean Evergreen?"

"Evergreen!" exclaimed Mr. Grit. "That's the one."

Edwina suddenly put two and two together, the answers falling into her head. "You mean to say…"

"That I was behind that?" he laughed. "Yes! Yes, I was. And it went so wonderfully to plan. I was perched over the mountains, looking down over the village — the moment the silly little blight reached the top of the tree I used my magic and shot him down, down to the ground, where he banged his head and forget about Christmas. Admittedly, he didn't forget as much as I would have liked him to have done son, but that was easily fixed. I got my assistant, Crook — a former Elf himself of the North Pole, until he was Banished — to take on a disguise. He's currently pretending to be a new Elf called Kane, with Evergreen being under the impression he is there to help Evergreen upon his return to work and that Evergreen can help Kane in his training — a perfect combination, a perfect excuse. We've slipped him a potion that modifies memory — right now, let's just say we've got him exactly where we want him."

"And where's that?" Edwina asked, eagerly, standing up. This had gained her interest, that was for sure, and now she had heard all this, she needed to know the full story; she needed to know more, the inner reporter, the inner journalist, that she was, consuming her.

Mr. Grit stopped talking for a moment, letting the suspense build. He had yet to be able to tell anybody what he was up to, and yet now this was his time, his moment, his chance to see somebody react to his plan for the first. He let the moment drag for another moment, so much so Edwina could barely stand it another second longer.

"We've broken into the list of The Naughty and The Nice."

Edwina gasped. She didn't even mean to. But breaking into the List — that wasn't even skirting around the HQ, trying to upset the North Pole slowly at first, or being subtle about trying to bring down Father Christmas — that was right to the heart of all matters.

"You broke into it?" she asked; she couldn't help but admit she was impressed.

Mr. Grit was savouring her reaction. It was the best reaction he could have hoped for, if not better. "That we did. Kane and Evergreen went into work today, after Evergreen had consumed the memory potion. Kane told him they needed to get the key and do an inspection of the List Department. Evergreen thought that's what they've been asked to do, and so he did it. He's a good worker, but he's also a goody two shoes. He'll do anything he's told, as long as he's been convinced it's something that's acceptable, something that's allowed."

"And then what happened?"

"Kane mixed some of the names up. Changed some of the labels. Swapped around a few of the pages — and those pages are big, and the writing on them is small. So small. They're put under special magnifying glasses that are some of the most powerful in the world just to be able to read it — I mean, there's over seven billion people in the world. Can you imagine how much space and paper you'd need if the writing was normal sized? Plus, Elves have far better eyesight than humans anyway — they're able to read much smaller prints. Better to be able to read the small labels on the toys."

Edwina was nodding along, but her mind had begun to wander as soon as Mr. Grit had begun describing to her the intricate details about small print and eyesight. She was more interested in the break-in, more intrigued about the consequences, more delighted over the thought of just how much chaos it would cause.

"What's going to happen next?" she asked.

"Well," Mr. Grit said, stroking his chin. "We've thought about it long and hard — we're not going to make a song and dance about it. It'll be far better to just leave it to play out. The closer we get to Christmas Eve, the bigger the chance everything will be messed up."

"And if they find out the room has been broken into?"

"Then they'll have to figure out if the List has been tampered with or not, won't they? But they only make the one list — it's not like it's electronic, or they write multiple copies they can compare it against, is it? They'll just have to hope for the best. Fools!" he added, the prospect of the trouble he'd caused striking him once more, playing out in his imagination.

Edwina couldn't help but laugh. "It is very impressive, I have to admit. But, and I apologise, but I still don't understand why you're here. Why are you telling me this? It's not like this is something I'm going to be able to print in The Northerly Herald."

"Well I know that!" hollered Mr. Grit. "I've just confided in a crime I've committed to you — how big of a fool do you take me for if you think I want you to print it for the world to see?"

"Exactly," Edwina said, agreeing. "That's what I mean. So how can I help you?"

"Like I said, I want to make a deal with you."

"A deal?"

"A deal."

"What type of a deal?" Edwina asked, taking a seat again.

"I want us to join forces. I've got Crook and Evergreen and magic and potions all on my side. You've got a group of Goblins, yes? They're already inside the HQ — and whilst I know they're doing a good job, and so are you, so please don't think I'm trying to say you're not. But what I am saying is this: I've got an Elf — an Elf who knows the HQ inside out; like the back of his hand, and we've got him to our advantage. Together, we can take over that place. We've got a team between the two of us, we've got an expert, we've got an assistant, and we've got your newspaper."

"Nobody is touching my newspaper," Edwina said, suddenly getting defensive. "That's my livelihood and my life's work right here. Nobody else is going to help me run it."

Mr. Grit shook his head. "No, no, no," he said. "I'm not saying I want to help you run it. What I'm saying is: it's very impressive, and it's very popular, and it's something that between the two us, we have it to our advantage, because you can bring it to the table. Together, think of all the mischief we could cause. Together, think of all the truths we could expose. Together, think about how powerful we could be."

Edwina sat there, quietly, chewing her lip in thought. She was a powerful lady, she knew. She had always known that if she worked hard enough she could have anything she wanted, and so far in her life she had always succeeded in doing this. She was unsure whether to work with someone else, whether to split the responsibility, but she knew it could speed things up, and she knew together, combining their forces and their assets, they could do twice as much damage, and uncover twice as many truths. She could have more material for The Northerly Herald. Sales could boom with more people snatching up copies, meaning more money than she had ever made before. It was a small sacrifice of responsibility and ownership for a reward that was huge in comparison.

As a businesswoman, she knew it was a no-brainer.

She stood up, smoothing her fingers down her dress, and stepping forward, her high-heels clicking against the floor, and then came to a stop in front of Mr. Grit.

Sticking her hand out, she spoke. “You’ve got yourself a deal.”

Mr. Grit broke into a grin.

“Deal.”

They shook hands, and the deal was made, their future sealed. They couldn’t have been happier.

30

FATHER CHRISTMAS WAS marching down the corridors of the HQ, eager to reach the Sleigh Department. He could feel his stress levels rising as he walked, thinking about all the delays this would cause, and trying to figure out who had done this — as if he hadn't got enough going on right now, as if there weren't enough material for people to gossip about and chat over, and now this.

He just knew how it would look. People would start believing what they were reading; they would start believing he was incapable of running the North Pole, not capable of being able to make sure Christmas was successful, not the right person to make sure everybody in the world was happy on Christmas Day. Just the thought of it upset him — he had spent his whole life wanting to do this job; this was all he had ever wanted to do, and all he ever wanted to be, and now he felt as though it was fading before his very eyes, under his very nose, and he didn't know how it was happening.

He knew the reports were false, but the events they had written about were true — Evergreen the Elf had fallen off the top of the Christmas tree and yet he still did not know how it had happened. The Sleigh Department had been broken into, and he didn't know how it had happened, when it had happened, who had done it or why, or even how the story had broke and gotten out to the newspapers before he had been notified of it. There were too many questions, and Father Christmas was beginning to doubt himself, beginning to start to believe the reports that were written about himself. Maybe they were right — maybe he wasn't the right one to run the HQ, maybe he wasn't the Father Christmas who should be in charge of Christmas, perhaps it was time for somebody who was more fresh, more on the ball, more on top of their game — somebody who could run it better than him and keep up with the demands of it all, especially as he knew year on year now Christmas would only continue to grow more stressful, become increasingly complex, even more demanding than every year before, as the world grew in size and the demands got bigger. Maybe it was best if he was to just resign…

He shook the thought firmly out of his head, telling himself off for ever believing such a thing. How could he had even considered quitting, and leaving the place behind? Even though he hadn't confided this thought in anybody else, he felt bad for even contemplating it within the private space of his own mind, and reminded himself that was the beginning of letting whoever it was who had something against them to win, and he wouldn't have it. He was too dedicated, and this place meant too much to him, and so did the people, and so did the world, and so did Christmas. He scolded himself and then focused on the mission in hand.

It wasn't until they reached the doors of the Sleigh Department, which now had two Security Goblins stood on either side of the double doors, that he came to a stop, his team surrounding him, and spoke again.

"Right," he said. "Time to have a look at what's gone on."

"Are you sure you want to, Sir?"

Father Christmas turned around, and looked at Mr. Jingelton. "What do you mean by that?"

Looking taken aback, Mr. Jingelton stemmed. "I, I… I just thought you might not want to see it. I..I was just thinking in case it upset you."

"I get that," Father Christmas said, "but I have to see it, so I can do something about it, don't I?"

Mr. Jingelton looked across at Goose for a bit of help, but none was given. Goose was quiet. He was thinking a lot more than he was letting on — watching all of this happen to Father Christmas was not only beginning to get him down, but it was starting to frustrate him too. Father Christmas, Goose both believed and knew, was a good person. He had always been a good person, somebody who had wanted to make a difference to the people and to help add a bit of magic, a bit of happiness, to the world. Now Goose felt as though it was all being taken away from beneath his feet, everything he had worked so hard for so long, and taken so much pride in, and he didn't know what or who, and he didn't like it. He knew there had to be some reason, that there had to be some explanation, some logic, behind it all, but right now all he had was a series of questions and no answers and a lot of frustration building up and nobody to take it out on. It was getting him down.

The double doors opened, the Security Goblins pulling them open and then standing back to let them in, and Goose followed behind Mr. Jingelton and Father Christmas. As soon as they stepped into the room, Goose gasped. Mr. Jingelton cursed his breath. Father Christmas was speechless. The two Security Goblins looked at one another, then walked back out the room, shutting the double doors close behind them with a thud.

The third reverberated around the room, and then the echo faded, leaving the three of them just stood there, in the entrance, looking at the sight in front of them, and completely unsure of what to say or do.

The Sleigh was scratched and graffitied. It now had parts missing. It had slits in the seats, and the cushions had been pulled open, the feathers from inside them, taken from geese, strewn across the floor. The reigns were broken, having been cut in half. The sack had been pulled open, and the depths of the warehouse inside could be seen — Father Christmas, although wishing this had never happened at all, kind of wished this had happened just a couple of days later, when the Sleigh Arrangement Department would have been working in the sack, because then maybe somebody might have heard something happening on the outside, caught or identified the guilty one, and then have put a stop to all this mess.

But it was too late for thinking of what could or should have happened.

"It's terrible," said Goose.

"I've never seen anything like it," added Mr. Jingelton.

They were both in shock. Father Christmas, however, appeared to be relatively calm.

"Right," he said, clapping his hands together. "We need a POA."

"A 'p' of what?" Mr. Jingelton asked.

Goose rolled his eyes. "You should know that."

"Well, I am sorry! I'm sure we've got more pressing things right now that knowing — "

"Plan of Action, it means," Father Christmas said, cutting them both off. "We need a Plan of Action. I'm going to send you both to order new parts and materials for the sleigh. I don't care how much it costs or how difficult it is to get them ordered or made — I need a sleigh, and I need one that works, and I need one pretty soon, so that's top priority. Anything else that needs doing, you ignore it. Do I make myself clear?"

They both nodded.

"I'm going to try and find out who did this. I knew I should have agreed to having cameras put up around the place, but I thought this was the North Pole — a place of magic and happiness and of people who wanted to do good for the world and the people within it. I never, not once, not in a million years, thought that something like this could happen in a place like this." He shook his head from side to side, and both Goose and Mr. Jingelton saw that he didn't look angry or mad or cross, but instead he just looked tired; he looked worn-out, dismayed, disappointed, and that was probably worse than seeing him shouting and being incredibly bad-tempered over the recent incidents.

"Maybe…" he started, stopping with a sigh. "Maybe I think I need to have a reconsider."

He took another look over the mess that covered the room, the state of the sleigh, and sighed once more with another shake of the head. He raised his hand up, as though he was trying to push it away, then exhaled and turned around. Before they knew it, he was walking out of the room, without another word, and vanishing from sight. Goose and Mr. Jingelton thought it would be best if they didn't ask where he was going or what he was planning on doing, but rather just leave him to it instead.

They looked at each, shrugged and shook their own heads at one another, then pulled out their notebooks and pens and got wandering around the sleigh, inspecting it up close and writing up what parts needed re-fitting, replacing, or repairing.

There were a lot of them, that was for sure.

31

EVERGREEN WAS CONFUSED.

He was sat at home, on the sofa, by himself. His head felt so fuzzy, so strange — he had never felt like this before in his life. He had never got drunk before, alcohol only rarely being permitted in the North Pole, and only during specific times of the year in orders of celebrations, but he imagined this would be what it felt like to have drunk too much and then not remember much from the night before.

Everything felt disjointed — he kept remembering flashes of certain scenes, bits of memories, but have difficulty to string them all together to make one long sequence that actually made logical sense. He could recall, that morning, going into work with Kane — just the same as he had done the morning before. He could remember starting his work, and then Kane telling him they had been given a special task to do — a task that only the two of them had been asked to do.

Then the next thing he knew, they had both been in the Sleigh Department. He couldn't remember how he had gotten there, but he did remember holding a golden key in his hand — which surely meant he hadn't done anything wrong. He knew enough to know the HQ kept their keys — well, they kept their keys under lock and key. It wasn't as though just any old fool could come along and grab a key and off they go to wherever they please — you only get given a key if you need a key, and are allowed a key — and so he must have been granted permission.

But then, before he knew it, he had been surrounded by mess and disaster and destruction. A scene flashed before his eyes; it was of him backing out of the room, his eyes canning the place over, looking at what had happened, wondering how it had happened, why it had happened, and what would happen next. He could remember the panic running through his veins, the adrenaline suddenly kicking in as he had realised what had happened and how he had played a part in it — but then the next thing…

The next thing…

Well, that was where it all went hazy. All went fuzzy and cloudy and unclear. He couldn't get his brain to work. It felt as though he was trying to get the cogs to turn but they'd been turned rusty and then covered in golden syrup to slow them down even more, just for good measure. He could remember signing a signature to agree not to talk to anybody about what had happened, but he knew that didn't seem right in itself.

The more he thought about everything though, the more he tried to make sense of it all, the more all of the memories seemed to be fading from his mind. The morning seemed to be running away from him, collecting the key appeared to be fading, the department he had been in appeared to be swirling into some vortex where memories and thoughts become unreachable, forgotten about for eternity.

Before he knew it, he did a burp — little did he know it was from the potion — and then he shook his head, blinked several times, and then wondered what it was he was doing. He felt ill, and as though he had been involved in some sort of a fight, because his head felt as though it had been hit round the back. It was thumping, and he felt awfully tired. For a moment, he considered calling somebody up to come round so that he wasn't by himself, but he didn't know what he would tell them, didn't know what he would expect them to do.

No, he decided. They would think he had gone mad — think something worse had happened to him when he fell from the top of the Christmas tree, and then he'd be sent away again. They'd say that his head injury was worse than they thought. They'd keep him in hospital and he'd miss Christmas. They'd talk and amongst themselves decide it would be best if he was kept out of the HQ, not allowed to go and work anymore. The thought of it all filled his entire body up with dread — he wouldn't allow.

He would keep quiet.

He would keep quiet about the way he was feeling, and he would keep quiet about what he had been through — except whatever it was that he had been through, he wasn't too sure, but he knew something — something — had happened.

But poor Evergreen just couldn't put his finger down onto what the something was…

32

THE GOBLINS WERE walking to The Northerly Herald from one side of town.

On the other side of town, Mr. Grit and Crook were also making their way to The Northerly Herald.

Neither the Goblins nor Crook knew what for, or even that it was The Northerly Herald they were heading.

"Where are we going?" Crook asked, following along behind Mr. Grit. The weather was absolutely bitter, nearly at the height of Christmas, and snow had started falling from the sky, creating a new white blanket atop of what had just turned into compacted ice over the last few weeks, from all the footsteps of the hustle and bustle of the townsfolk, preparing themselves for Christmas, and dashing here and there. He was also tired — today at the HQ hadn't been easy, what with not only breaking into the Sleigh Department, but worrying about Evergreen and how well the potion worked. Crook had been constantly on edge, worrying that it would fail and that Evergreen would end up telling somebody what they'd done.

"You'll find out in a minute," Mr. Grit replied.

"Well, why can't I find out now?"

"Because I said so, that's why."

"But that's not a reason."

Mr. Grit rolled his eyes. "You sound like a child. A whinging child."

"Tell me then!""

"I can't! If somebody sees us and overhears, I'll get more people into trouble."

"More pe—"

"Hush!" exclaimed Mr. Grit, batting his hands in the air and flailing at Crook. "What did I just say? I don't want to talk about it out here. I don't want that risk."

"Okay, okay" Crook said back, exasperated. He hadn't seen Mr. Grit act like this before — he seemed to be a strong combination of extremely excited but also extremely on edge too. It didn't make much sense. And what had he meant by more people? Did this mean there were others who were going to be joining their operation?

He hoped not. Well, half of him hoped not. In one sense, it would be nice for the heat to be taken off of him, if Mr. Grit could have other people who could help him out on the mission, to spread the responsibility around. But then, in another sense, he hadn't really thought about just how much he had invested in this operation so far, not until now when he contemplated the thought it might be taken away from him. Crook realised he suddenly didn't like this thought.

But, either way, no matter what he thought, he didn't have to wait very long to find out. They made their way out of town, trudging through the snow where it came thicker, the temperature colder and the snow harsher now that they were out in the elements, and they didn't stop nor speak until a building came into view in the distance.

It was all red brick with black-out windows, and Crook thought it looked smarter and modern, rather futuristic. It had a strip of screen running across it, small text zipping from one side to the other, and as they got closer and Crook squinted his eyes to see what the words were saying, he realised they were headlines. Another screen had different times on it, and he understood these to be the different timezones from around the globe. In huge, white letters were the words THE NORTHERLY HERALD, and it suddenly clicked into place at just what this building was — and then Crook felt himself become confused.

"What are we coming here for?"

Mr. Grit didn't stop walking, instead now walking faster than ever as though he was a man on a mission — which, Crook supposed, he essentially was — but turned his head back round to give Crook a stern look.

"You're being terribly impatient," he complained. "Everything will make sense when we're inside."

"You're not going to tell the papers what's happened, are you?"

Mr Grit scowled at this. "And just why would I do that? Do you really think I would be so stupid. Do you really think I would turn myself in?"

"No," Crook said, quickly. "I wasn't saying that. I just meant —
"

"I don't care," Mr. Grit snapped. "I don't want to know. I think I know what I'm doing, so do as you're told and just wait a few minutes. Yes?"

Crook just nodded, but didn't say anything.

Mr. Grit didn't bother trying to get a response, and not that he had much time to, either. As they finished talking, when they were nearly at the double-doors, automatic and made out of glass, a bunch of chattering suddenly broke into the night and they both stopped in their tracks.

Suddenly, a gaggle of Goblins rounded the corner, walking and bouncing and trudging along, some looking happy and some looking dopey and some looking moody to be here, and even, Crook noticed, a couple of them looked nervous to be here, and then came to an immediate stop the moment they looked up and saw Mr. Grit and Crook staring at them.

They just started back.

A moment of nothingness happened, where both parties just stood looking at one another, neither being the first to speak, neither quite knowing how to process what was stood before their eyes, when the double-doors slid open, and out walked Edwina Inksmith.

She looked from her left to her right, from the group of Goblins to the tall villain and his short sidekick, and then back again. "Did you all get the wrong memo?" she asked. "I said the meeting was inside, not out here." She laughed at her own joke and then slipped what must have been a cigarette that she was going to smoke back into the pocket of her coat. She did it quickly, obviously hoping nobody would notice what she had been holding. It didn't work — Mr. Grit picked up on it right away.

"I notice everything," he said.

"What do you mean?" she asked.

"The cigarette," he replied. "I didn't know you smoked."

"I don't."

"Decoration, then?" he retorted.

"I don't very often," she remarked.

He raised his eyebrows. She pursed her lips.

Crook cleared his throat, and they both broke away their staring game with one another, looking around.

"Sorry," Edwina said, blushing slightly, although she wasn't quite too sure why. "If you'd all like to follow me, and I'll take you inside. I know we've all got a lot we need to talk about."

Everybody looked from one to the other, all of them feeling rather skeptical about whatever it was they were about to hear, and then followed Edwina into the depths of The Northerly Herald.

As they walked through the double-doors, they were met with a wall of hot air that hit them and enveloped around them, a warm welcome in contrast to the coldness outside. The building was bigger on the inside than it appeared to be on the outside. From the ground floor, if you were to tilt your head back and look up, you could see all the way up to the ceiling. The floors ran around the edges, the corridors more like huge balconies, and then the offices ran all the way around the edges, the walls of them glass so that you could see in and out of them from the corridors and the offices. The elevators were glass, too, and they looked smart and modern as they all headed towards them. The colouring of the furnishings were black, white and silver, and it all looked so sleek. Here and there were dotted comfy-looking chairs and tables and beanbags, as well as computers and notebooks — the perfect place for anybody who wanted to sit and talk a report over, or focus and write down a story quickly, so it could be published and printed and put out there as fast as they possibly could.

Packing all into the glass lift, Edwina closed the doors with a touch of a button, then pressed another button that lit up white with a small, delicate ping.

“My office is at the top,” she explained, as the elevator began to rise. But we’re going to be in the conference suite today.”

As she finished speaking, the doors opened and she stepped out, her high-heels clicking against the floor as she marched away and led them all to the conference suite, everyone scurrying after her as fast she could. She certainly could walk very fast, whilst giving the impression she was also very graceful and moved slowly. It was a signature of the way that she worked too — she liked to think she could be powerful, that she was powerful, and yet she didn’t have to make a song and a dance about it to be so. Edwina Inksmith had always said she much rather her work spoke for itself, than needing her to be a major character to get it out there and bring it to life — and, that attitude, so far, had worked.

"Here we go," she said. "Help yourself to food."

The Goblins all looked at one another excitedly at the sound of food, and then nearly burst from excitement when they saw a buffet had been made up for them all — it was full of dozens of different types of cheeses, sandwiches, crisps and puddings, from custard slices to jam tarts to iced-finger buns. They began to race over, and then Gordon made a grumbling sound and called them back.

"Hang on, hang on, hang on!" he said, urgently, rounding them back up as though they were sheep that had been allowed to run wild. "We've been brought here on important business. I think food can wait for a moment, don't you?"

The Goblins just stood and stared, looking between Edwina and Gordon and the buffet, clearly unsure of which one they should pick. Glancing between one another, they grumbled to themselves and then made their way to the front of the conference suit, taking their seats and trying their best to forget about the growling sounds their stomaches were making, and to push the image of all the different delicacies and treats out of their memories. It had been a long time since they had eaten. This already put them all into a bad mood, and an even worse one with Gordon. When he came to sit down next to them, they all shuffled up, leaving a gap between him and them. He rolled his eyes at their pettiness, and folded his arms, looking towards the front of the room instead and pretending he didn't care — which, in all fairness, he didn't.

Mr. Grit and Crook took a look at one another, and then sat down on a row of chairs on the other side of the aisle of the conference suite, as Edwina walked through the middle and then stood at the front, behind a little podium. Crook looked out of the glass wall, and through it you could see the other floors of The Northerly Herald, including Edwina's office on the other side of the same floor. It was a perfect spot for it to be, he realised, because it provided Edwina with a great view into pretty much every floor — which meant she could make sure everyone was working when they should be at any time she fancied, and they couldn't hide from her. A perfect layout plan for Edwina, most likely a terrible one for her workers sometimes.

Edwina began to talk, and Mr. Grit elbowed him in the ribs, making him turn quickly back around and up to the front of the room. He felt as though he was back in school and had been told off for speaking during class.

"Now then," Edwina said, her voice surprisingly soft, and Crook couldn't help but think that this wasn't how she usually spoke, but rather it was because she was trying to talk them into something. "I think it's time for some introductions, don't you?" She smiled. Her audience smiled back. "On the left, we have Mr. Grit and his assistant, Crook. On the right, we have Gordon and my team — and his team — of Goblins, who are journalists. Now, without either of us knowing, we both have something in common."

They all shuffled on their seats, edging forwards slightly, eager to hear what the news was that Edwina was about to spill.

"We've all intercepted with the daily on-goings of operations within the HeadQuarters of the North Pole, affecting Father Christmas and his team, and subsequently Christmastime in general."

They was a gasp in the room. Crook looked at the Goblins, and the Goblins looked back at Mr. Grit and Crook.

"Yes, yes," Edwina said, smiling, clearly taking delight in being the one to break this story, the inner journalist coming out of her. "I know, I know, it's shocking. Mr. Grit has been in charge of an operation, and — as you know — I've been running my own. But today. Well, today, together, Mr. Grit and I made a deal."

The Goblins nearly fell off their seats. Crook almost stood up. Mr. Grit and Edwina looked at one another — this had been what they had been worried about. Actually, tell a lie — they weren't actually too fussed; they knew they'd make them do what they wanted in the end anyway, but it was all about the way they were perceived, the way that the others saw them — and so they had to look worried, so that they could look as though they cared about what the others thought to their plans.

"What sort of a deal?" Crook asked.

"A good one," Edwina said, with a smile.

"In what way?" asked Gordon.

"All in good time," replied Mr. Grit.

"We want to know now!" hollered one of the Goblins, standing up and raising his fist into the air. The others stood up and joined in, cheering and jeering.

"All right, all right, all right!" exclaimed Edwina, flapping her hands up and down. “Calm down and we can speak. How am I supposed to say anything constructive if I have to talk over a bunch of wild baboons?”

The Goblins look shocked at the insult, but sat down nonetheless, albeit grumbling once again and muttering under their breaths to one another as they did so.

“Baboon, my bottom,” one of them said.

“She wouldn’t know a baboon if it stared her in the face.”

Edwina cleared her throat. Silence fell across the room.

“It doesn’t really make too much of a difference — our plans aren’t changed; what we’ve planned is still saying the same. Just Mr. Grit’s assistant has — let’s say, befriended — a worker in the HQ. He’s an Elf — the very same Elf who fell from the top of the Christmas tree at the start of the month.”

“The one who bumped his head?” asked a Goblin.

“Evergreen?” added Gordon.

“Evergreen,” smiled Edwina, nodding. “Crook has befriended Evergreen, although I am lead to believe Evergreen believes Crook is called Kane within the HQ, am I correct?”

Mr. Grit and Crook nodded at the same time.

“Just as I thought,” Edwina said, then turned back to face the room. “Christmas Eve is fast approaching and we can use Evergreen to our advantage — until this mission, none of us have ever been in the HQ before. Evergreen, however, obviously has. He knows the HQ like the back of his head — he could probably navigate his way around it with a blindfold tied around his head. This is what we need. This is what would benefit us the most."

One of the Goblins raised their hands, a confused expression across his face.

"Yes, Bletchley?"

"What if Evergreen tells someone what we're up to?"

"He won't."

"But what if?"

"But he won't."

"But how do you know?"

"Because I do!" she shouted back. "Because I know, and that should be enough of an answer. I know why he won't, and I think if I'm happy with something, then you all should be do too. Now that's enough of the questions."

"Only asked one..." muttered one Goblin.

"And enough of the cheek, too," she added, pursing her lips. "Now, we need to turn our attention to Christmas Eve. Christmas Eve is fast approaching, and we need to decide what we're going to do on it — or rather, how we're going to go about doing what we're going to be doing.

"Now," she continued, "we need to stop Father Christmas from delivering those presents. Mr. Grit and Crook have already sustained some damage to the the List of the Naughty and the Nice, and so that should make sure things are delayed within the HQ. At the same time, don't forget that Father Christmas starts his trial at court tomorrow —

something he really doesn't have the time for, but which he has to do nonetheless, whether he likes it or not. Now, nobody can interrupt him whilst he's in court, and his Head Team — Goose and Mr. Jingelton, as I think they're more commonly known by in the HQ — have to be there with him, too, as I believe they are also being questioned by the Court.

"This means," Edwina said, standing up a little straighter, "that the HQ will be without any leaders or people with power or knowledge within the HQ. Now, I think this is a rather foolish move, but — then again — they probably never expected that all of their leadership team would be with the Court all on the same day — or at all, for that matter. It's certainly a new one in the history books. So this means we need to use that day — which is the day before Christmas Eve — to cause disruption. We're going to get Evergreen a promotion — to the Sleigh Department, and he's going to delay it. Crook is going to pretend to fix the List, but he's not really going to. You Goblins are going to cause mischief — knock over a few toys, swipe the carrots from the reindeers, hassle Father Christmas with false problems on Christmas Eve — anything to delay him. Gordon is going to be in charge of you all whilst you're in the HQ, as I obviously won't be there. I'll be here, keeping The Northerly Herald running and dripping news of the disruptions to the public, because Gordon is going to report the stories to me first.

"So," she said, drawing to a close, "that's everything. Nothing too hard to do, but we have to all work together to pull it off. Snowflakes can add up to being snowed in. We need to be the snowstorm. Do I make myself clear?"

The thought of it all swirled around everyone's minds, thinking about the enormity of what they were going to do. They had never heard of anything as big as this before in history when it came to trying to bring the North Pole down. Half of them were sure there was no way they were going to be able to do it, but if it's one thing Goblins and Elves are, it's stubborn — and none of them were about to say no, or let Edwina down.

Edwina and Mr. Grit looked at one another as the Goblins broke into conversation, discussing the next forty-eight hours ahead. They nodded at each other and gave one another a discreet smile.

The snowstorm was on the way. It just needed to stay on the same course.

33

FATHER CHRISTMAS WAS nervous, and he was never nervous, and it wasn't just because it was the night before Christmas Eve.

The only times he had ever let himself feel anxious was Christmas Eve, but only right before take-off, and not because he was scared of flying, but because it was only then it ever truly dawned on him on just how big of a task he was about to undertake. The pressure that he had to get everything done in one night; the pressure knowing that it was up to him to make sure everybody had a smile on their face come the morning; the pressure to reach more people than the year before. But it was always worth it.

As soon as he was up in the air, the clouds rushing by as the sleigh skimmed through the surface of them, under the blue of the night, the silver stars glittering overhead, and the towns and the lakes and the fields, blanketed in snow, speeding down below him, he felt free, and happy, and he was reminded why he would do this forever if he could, was reminded that it was always worth it, reminded that this was the best thing in the world, that he would continue working every year to make Christmas the best it could be, to make sure that every Christmas time was better than the Christmas time before.

But, right now, all of that felt as though it was in jeopardy. This morning was the morning of the court case, and Father Christmas was not looking forward to it. He had never been summoned to court before, and now that he was, he felt as though everybody was watching, and he didn't feel as though everybody believed him. The truth of it was that it was made even worse because even he didn't know the answers. He didn't know why Evergreen had fallen off the top of the Christmas tree. He didn't know if it was the fault of his Security Department. He didn't know if it had been an issue with the tree. He didn't know how the news had gotten out about the sleigh. He didn't even know who had been responsible for the destruction of it.

There were just so many things he didn't know, and he didn't like it, because he was supposed to be the person in charge, he was supposed to be the boss — the person that everybody looked up to when they needed answers, when they needed to be helped, when they needed support, and right now he felt as though he was just as clueless as everybody else, and he hated it — he hated that he was beginning to look as though he was a failure, when he had always taken pride in making sure he was the leader everybody deserved, making sure he was the Father Christmas that Christmas time deserved, and instead he felt as though he was just letting everybody down. All the years he had worked to make Christmas, Christmas. But now he felt as if it was all beginning to crumble in his fingertips and no matter how much he tried to keep a grasp on it, it was turning into sand and falling away from him, quicker than he was able to catch any of it.

He stood back in the mirror, and Mrs. Christmas stood back too. He exhaled, his belly expanding, and then he ran his fingers down his blazer.

"I think you look very smart."

"I think I look a fool."

Mrs. Christmas smiled a small, sad smile. "Well, I would have to disagree. You look handsome."

Father Christmas took another glance at himself in the mirror, then let his head drop. He caught his wife looking at his reflection behind him, and then he suddenly felt a pang of guilt hit him. He hadn't stopped to think this morning about how she would be feeling.

"Sorry," he said, pulling his eyes away from the reflection and turning to face Mrs. Christmas. He took her hands into his, and squeezed them in his palms.

"What for?" she said, quietly, so quiet it was almost a whisper.

"For being the way I am," he replied, almost just as quiet. "For this morning. For this month. For everything, I suppose."

Mrs. Christmas squeezed his hands back, and then freed one of her hands and tapped him on the nose. "I won't have it," she said, shaking her head side to side, looking up at him with a determined look on her face. "I won't hear a word of apology from you. None of this is your fault — and I know that, deep down, you know that, too. I know you feel responsible, and I get it — honestly, I do — but please, please remember it isn't. You're just as clueless as everybody else."

"But that's the thing," Father Christmas retorted back, quickly.

"That's my problem — because I'm not everybody else. I'm Father Christmas. I'm supposed to be the one running this place. I'm supposed to be the one with all the answers. What good is it if I can't even help my own people out? Out of all the days they could do it, why does it have to be today? Why do it so close to Christmas Eve?" He finished, and then his head sunk again, his expression falling.

Mrs. Christmas had never seen him look this way before, had never seen him look so defeated. Even when the HQ had been busy, even when the deadlines had become tighter and the production numbers gotten bigger, and his stress levels had risen with them, he had always just looked determined instead, taken it in his stride and looked excited to take on the challenge instead.

But now?

Now he looked tired, worn, stressed and defeated, and Mrs. Christmas knew this wasn't the Father Christmas she knew.

"Everything will turn out okay in the end," she said. "I promise." But even as she said the words, she knew it was a promise she couldn't truly keep — she, too, was just as clueless as everybody else. She had no clue how the day would turn out. She had no clue what evidence would come out. She guessed only time would tell.

"Are you sure you don't want me there today?" she asked. "For support."

Father Christmas shook his head. "No, no," he said. "It's Christmas Eve tomorrow — the HQ will be busy, who knows what type of problems could arise. I need you to hold the fort."

Mrs. Christmas nodded. “I understand.” Since Father Christmas, as well as both Mr. Jingelton and Goose, would all be at the Court today, Mrs. Christmas was going to be taking over as head of the HQ, and running all operations for the day. She still had a lot of last minute letters and admin to do, but there was no other choice — there was nobody else left who was qualified to run the place, and so despite being strained and spread thin, it was just what they were going to have to do.

Looking down at his golden wristwatch, Father Christmas sighed and then looked up. “I guess I have to get going.”

Mrs. Christmas took a glance at her own watch, and then nodded. “Yes,” she said. “You don’t want to be late. I’ll walk you out.”

They began walking, and then Father Christmas came to a sudden stop.

“What’s wrong?” Mrs. Christmas asked.

“I just want to say…” he broke off.

“Say what?”

But he just shook his head, and took her into a hug, then planted a kiss on her lips.

“What was that for?” she asked with a smile.

“Does a man need a reason to show affection to his wife?”

“I suppose not,” laughed Mrs. Christmas.

“But it’s just to say thank you for being there — thank you for your support and for being in this with me.”

Mrs. Christmas laughed. “I couldn’t think of a better job or a better place to be. Me and you?" she said. "Me and you are in this together. We have been since the start, and we will be until the end. Do I make myself clear, sweetheart?"

Father Christmas smiled back. "You do." He gave her another hug, and then together they walked out of the door and into the HQ.

34

THE COURT OF the Naughty and the Nice was an impressive Department.

It was within the HQ, but Father Christmas let it run independently, but walking into it he could understand why the people who were tested and trialed there felt overwhelmed. The ceiling was high, stretching up into the air, where a glass dome was set into it. It was a dull day outside, the sky a dark grey in colour. Lights were on in the Court, orange in colour, it made it feel like the middle of the night.

Circular in shape, the Court was set in the centre of benches that rose up and ran all the way around it, so that when Father Christmas took his seat next to Goose and Mr. Jingelton, and their lawyer, he felt as though he was sat in the middle of a circus. He hadn't been too sure just how many people would turn up to watch him in Court, to see how the trial played out, what with it being Christmas Eve and people being busy, but nearly every single seat was full. In fact, the more he scanned his eyes around the room, the more he noticed that in actual fact he couldn't find an empty seat. It was as though the entire town had come out to watch the trial — he was almost convinced that there was nobody actually in the HQ, that nobody was working for the deadline of Christmas, that there were nobody for Mrs. Christmas to even manage.

This stressed him out even more than it should have done — he knew he should just be focused on the court case, on the verdict, on the evidence they would present, the result that they would give, but no matter how much he tried to focus, his mind just kept wandering back to the HQ, wondering what was going on back there, hoping everything was okay, stressing in case nothing was running smoothly, frantically thinking something would be going wrong and he wasn't there, able to fix it. There were seven billion people tonight he had to please, and right now he was worrying if he'd be able to make any of them happy. What if he was late? What if he couldn't succeed? What if something drastic went wrong?

He gulped. Even worse, what if the Court stopped him from working and performing his duties?

He shook his head side to side. No, he told himself. That wouldn't happen. He wouldn't let it happen.

But, at the same time, no matter how much he told himself this, he knew he didn't have much choice in the matter, that for the first time this was something in which he truly had no control over, he wasn't used to it, he didn't like it, and the thought of it all scared him, even though he knew that he had done nothing wrong, but how could he prove that?

The truth was, unless something happened that proved otherwise, then he couldn't prove that — and that was the harsh reality of it, the harsh reality he was having trouble facing.

Just then, the Judge walked into the room. It was Judge Harper

— a very well respected Judge, with greying hair tied into a tight-bun and thin spectacles perching on the end of her nose. Her eyes were piercing blue and scanned around the room like a bird of prey. Even if you had never seen her before, it was more than obvious that this was a person who never missed a thing, that nothing could slip from her attention or run away from under her nose. She knew everything — that's the aura she gave about her — even if there was no possibility that she could know it, she would — somehow — already know it, and there was no arguing with her about the fact.

The Courtroom fell quiet with her entrance, and she gave a nod and a small smile of satisfaction upon greeting her colleagues and the courtroom. "Thank you," she said, her voice as sharp as her expression, as her eyesight. "You may now sit."

Everybody did as they were told, and they did so with efficiency, nobody wanting to be the last one to be stood up incase Judge Harper saw it as somehow disrespecting her. There were just were something about her that made everybody nervous, whether you were guilty or not, whether you were under trial or not, and whether she was a Judge or not.

"We are here today," she started, her eyes glossing over a file that was open in front of her, "to discuss the events which happened on the night of December the First, in which a young Elf, who goes by the name Evergreen, apparently — or supposedly, for the want of a better word — fell the top of the Christmas tree. A Christmas tree, which might I add, for those of who in the jury box today, had been modified to ensure that it was the largest Christmas tree that the North Pole had seen before in the Town Square. This is a tradition that has been followed for many years, to always ensure that the Christmas tree in question is larger than the year before, which resulted in the fact that this year's had to be subject to unnatural modifications to ensure that it reached that dizzying height."

"When Evergreen reached the top of the Christmas tree, after being selected Star Elf, which — for those of you who are unsure about what this means — is essentially being the Elf of the Year; for clarity this is a reward of recognition for your dedication and services to Father Christmas and the North Pole, in the business of the preparations for Christmas Eve and the delivery of tens of billions of presents to nearly seven billion people — which is also a number that continues to grow year on year, and a factor that I believe must be taken into consideration when we are considering this case."

"Why, you must ask. Well, the reason behind this is simply because how could we ignore the fact that the number of staff working within the North Pole HeadQuarters continue to remain, on average, the same, despite the number of people and the number of presents which are put on demand of Mr. Christmas and his team at the North Pole HeadQuarters year on year. Surely, this type of additional pressure must have some sort of an affect on the staff and the workers at the North Pole HeadQuarters — we all know it is a huge operation, and none of us would like to belittle the enormity nor the importance of what Mr. Christmas and the team of the North Pole HeadQuarters continue to do year on year, either."

At hearing this, Father Christmas exhaled slightly. No matter what happened, he felt as though this was a good sign — a small sign, admittedly, but a good sign nonetheless. It meant she recognised he was trying to do good, and that might mean that she believed in him.

"However, this leads to the natural questioning of what the North Pole HeadQuarters are considering in proposing to changing this, and to addressing this growing issue. Within business, if demand grows, it is a natural consequence and a natural reaction to expand your workforce in order to be able to better and more successfully cope with the growing demands that is not only expected of the workforce, but also of the individual worker, the individual employee, who must therefore work harder than the year previous in order to be able to make more items, in this case, more gifts. Surely this can only happen for so long — it is nonsensical to believe that there is no breaking point in which this trend can no longer be sustained. It is foolish to believe that the same number of employees can continue to produce an increasingly higher and higher number of presents without there being some type of a breaking point — where do you draw the line, and what is going to be done about?"

Goose shuffled in his seat, wanting to answer. The honest answer was that they hadn't really considered it — the Elf and the Goblin population weren't as advanced as the human population, and therefore growth hadn't taken place as much, but it was now beginning to slowly increase. The North Pole didn't let anybody enter — it was only people who were born in the North Pole who were able to work within the North Pole HeadQuarters — there were nowhere else where Elves or Goblins could live, after all. They were either born and lived and worked in the North Pole, or they were Banished and left, and moved somewhere else, they were the only two options to the people of the North Pole. Therefore, this meant that no matter how big the population of the world got, no matter how many presents they needed to make, no matter how many houses they needed to all be delivered to, if there were no more Elves or Goblins who were of age who could start work at the HQ, then the HQ just had to try their best. It wasn't ideal, but now that the Elf and Goblin population was increasing, they had been hoping that this would be something that would change going into the future.

"The answer, right now, does not matter, because that would only affect the future, and since no plan has been implemented, then it is not relevant. To the Court, and to the case, the only timeframe that is of importance is the time frame of that of the past. I think — and I also think I would be agreed with — that it is fair to suggest that this may not have happened if the workers were not as stretched thinly or under as much stress as they currently are subjected to, after our investigation has taken place."

Father Christmas, Goose, Mr. Jingelton, and their lawyer all sat forward. They felt as though this was going to be the time where they were going to hear something of importance. Was Judge Harper about to say something had been discovered? Father Christmas felt himself inhale again, and he could almost feel his heart thumping out of his chest underneath his black blazer and white shirt.

"The investigation, however, could not pinpoint a specific reason as to why this incident took place. We investigated the team that worked on the Christmas tree and the preparations for that night, with the Heath and Safety Department, and we did not find anything unusual. If anything, all safety precautions were taken, and all of them were ticked off on the tick-sheet, which is the same way that has been used every year. Therefore, we can say the incident was not caused by the Health and Safety Department. We then investigated the Magic and Modification Department, and the same can also be said for this Department in question — they, too, followed all procedures, all precautions, and successfully passed all their tests and ticked all of their own boxes on their own tick-sheets. Therefore, we can additionally say the incident was not caused by the Magic and Modification Department. Furthermore, we investigated the Security Department, and furthermore — once again — they too passed all the same tests, and — once again — ticked all of their own boxes on their own tick-sheets. Which does mean that we can say the incident was not caused by the Security Department.

"Whilst this is good news for the three aforementioned Departments, it is not good news for the Head Team — the Head Team made up of Father Christmas, and his two assistants whom sit before us today. The Court would like to reach the conclusion that we charge the Head Team of the North Pole HeadQuarters with failure to follow common business practice and ensure that their number of workers who are employed by them was expanded upon. This therefore meant that those who do work for them were subjected to harsher worker conditions, increasingly stressful shifts, and a dizzying number of responsibilities and tasks, which was ever increasing and was becoming even more difficult to reach, and would have presumably — if not, most definitely — become impossible to be sustained. This therefore means the Court feels the Head Team have not acted responsibly, and should therefore be suspended from their roles with the North Pole HeadQuarters for a yet-to-be-determined period of time."

"We will now go to the Jury to reach a verdict. So," Judge Harper said, turning away from the gaze of Father Christmas, Goose, Mr. Jingelton, and their lawyer, and turned to reach the ten people who were sitting in the Jury box — these were the ten people who would be the people who would make a decision by a number of votes as to whether Father Christmas, Goose, and Mr. Jingelton were guilty or not. "Those of who believe Father Christmas and his two assistants to be guilty and therefore to be charged, please rise."

But as to how many of them would rise, nobody would know, because before they had chance the doors of the Courts burst open and a Court official came running.

Everybody turned around to see what the commotion was all about.

"What is the meaning of this?" Judge Harper asked, sternly,

evidently not pleased at all about the arrival of such a disruption in her Courtroom, and at such a critical time too. If everybody had been on the edge of their breathes now, not daring to inhale or exhale out of suspense, then nobody dared to move now.

"I'm sorry, Judge Harper!" exclaimed the thin man who had a note in his hands. "But I must interrupt immediately —we've had an emergency. A Code Red."

Father Christmas quickly jumped up. Goose and Mr. Jingelton hurriedly followed suit.

"A Code Red?" he asked.

"That's correct, Sir," the man replied. "A Code Red."

"What's happened?" pressed Father Christmas.

"It's the List Department, Sir," said the main. "Or, more specifically, the List itself. It's been tampered with — the names are all over the place! If we don't get it sorted, then nobody will be getting any gifts tonight. We need to get this sorted and quickly, otherwise Christmas will be ruined for good!"

Father Christmas' eyes widened. "I'm well aware of what will happen, but thank you. This is dreadful." He span around to face Judge Harper. "I understand you need to do today, but…"

"There is no need to explain yourself, Mr. Christmas. The only thing this Court is ruled by is Code Reds. This case is suspended, to be picked back up at a more suitable time. Mr. Christmas, yourself and your team are dismissed. Everybody else, you may now rise and leave. Thank you."

Judge Harper picked up her hammer and hit it against the top of her desk, then rose herself and swept out of the Court. Father Christmas, Goose, and Mr. Jingelton thanked their lawyer, then went dashing out of the Court before anybody else had a chance to get up and leave themselves, and began their rush over to the List-room.

As they did so, nobody noticed that a Goblin who went by the name of Crook was slipping out of the audience too, and he himself went scurrying to communicate with Edwina Inksmith, so that they could be the first to report just what had gone on at The Northerly Herald — but they already knew they'd be the first. No other newspaper had been given access to the court case, and Edwina Inksmith couldn't wait to be the one to report what had gone on. It would mean guaranteed sales being the only newspaper to print the story, because everybody in the North Pole would want to know the juicy details, and so it was a winning situation for her.

Things couldn't be going more swimmingly.

35

FATHER CHRISTMAS, GOOSE, and Mr. Jingelton went dashing off out of the Court and running down the corridors as fast they could. It had been a long time since they last had a Code Red — so long, in fact, that Father Christmas couldn't even pinpoint exactly when the last one had happened, and neither Goose nor Mr. Jingelton had ever seen one during their careers at the HQ.

They reached the main hub of the HQ, and Father Christmas instantly slowed down and put his hands out.

"Why are we stopping?" Mr. Jingelton asked.

"We don't want to worry everyone," he answered.

"But they should be worried," Goose said. "Something terrible has happened."

"Until I know more answers," Father Christmas muttered out of the side of his mouth, "I don't know want anybody knowing a thing. I want it kept confidential until further notice, do I make myself understood?"

Then he went walking up ahead, quickening up his strides but not too quickly that it would raise any suspicions. Goose and Mr. Jingelton looked at one another as Father Christmas emptied the space between the two of them, and they just winded their eyes and shrugged their shoulders. Usually, Goose and Mr. Jingelton didn't see eye to eye, but on this one — well, they both felt equally as lost as the other.

Some of the Elves and Goblins within the HQ looked up as Father Christmas walked through the hustle and bustle of the place — it was completely frantic, what with it being the last day of work they had before tonight, what with it being so close to Christmas Eve. It was like Last Chance Saloon — anything they didn't get done now, then they'd never get done in time, and they knew that all that would result in is somebody waking up and finding themselves being unhappy in the morning, and the last thing anybody from the HQ wanted was for anybody to not be happy.

Some of them nodded or smiled at Father Christmas, acknowledging him as he made his way through them, and he greeted them back, making sure he too acknowledged all of them and all of the hard work they were doing. One of his best qualities about being a boss was that he brought an aura of calmness about him — importance, and authority, yes, but calmness too. If you weren't Mrs. Christmas, Goose, or Mr. Jingelton, then you would have presumed that hardly anything went wrong at the HQ, but if you were Mrs. Christmas, Goose, or Mr. Jingelton, then all you would know is that Father Christmas was really just an extraordinarily good actor — and right now was one of those times where he was acting extraordinarily well.

None of them stopped to speak until the madness had been left behind, after they had walked through several more corridors and took some more twists and turns, made their way through a series of doors, with Security Goblins — two at each door, with one at either side — now lining the way. An extra precaution that had obviously been ordered. Father Christmas presumed Mrs. Christmas was already down there, and that it was her very sensible calling to do this.

Sure enough, he was right, because as he stepped into the List Department, Mrs. Christmas came dashing over immediately. She look shocked, taken aback, but she, too, seemed calm, despite being pale.

"How's it going at Court?" she asked.

Father Christmas couldn't answer, instead just looking past her over at the List. He looked at her blankly, his mind obviously running at a million miles an hour, and then stepped past her.

She let out a quiet sigh. "How's it going at Court?" she repeated, this time asking Goose and Mr. Jingelton. Mr. Jingelton just shrugged his shoulders. Mrs. Christmas rolled her eyes, and looked expectantly at Goose.

"It's difficult to tell right now, if I be honest with you," he said. "They've recounted everything that's happened, and they've been discussing what's happened with each department that's been under investigation, but so far all it seems like is that they haven't found very much out."

"So when you do you find out the verdict?" she asked, eager to find out more, taking it all in.

"Well," Goose said, "they were just about to announce that before we got called here."

Mrs. Christmas clapped her hands to her mouth in surprise. "Why couldn't you have waited? You were so close to finding out!"

Goose shook his head. "They pronounced this a Code Red — and anything to do with Sir and a Code Red takes priority."

"Even over Court?"

"Even over Court," replied Goose.

Mrs. Christmas shook her own head, and then turned around. "It's chaos here," she said, looking over at the List, which Father Christmas was now examining a part of. There was pen all over it, arrows had been scribbled here and there, names crossed out and replaced on the other. Some names, Mrs. Christmas had noticed, had been completely removed full stop, and this was her main concern — with a lot of effort and a tonne of help, they might be able to decode the List and figure out which name should have gone where — but the names that had been scratched off? They're so much harder to be able to figure out now — so much so, that Mrs. Christmas was pretty sure nothing could be done. This was going to be it — this was going to be the end of Christmas as they knew it, and this was a thought that worried her, and not so much for herself, although it did scare her, but more because all she could think about is what it would do to her husband, what it would do to Father Christmas.

Christmas was his life. Christmas was what he was good at it. Christmas is what he was born to do. Without Christmas, Father Christmas would be lost, and without Father Christmas, Christmas itself would be lost. She shuddered just at the mere thought of it.

She attempted to push away those thoughts for now, but they were at the forefront of her mind, too difficult to ignore.

"I've got an idea," Father Christmas suddenly said, out of the blue, and when Mrs. Christmas blinked away the tears she had suddenly found in her eyes, she looked up to see Father Christmas coming into focus, a smile on his face.

A smile on his face? Had something gone wrong with her eyesight?

Goose and Mr. Jingelton both separately thought the same, presuming they must have been working far too long, that the stress of doing this job had all of a sudden caught up with them and become too much.

How could Father Christmas be smiling under a situation like this?

"An… an idea, love?" Mrs. Christmas asked, softly, thinking this was where it had all become too much for her husband too, that the stress of it had broken a fuse in his brain.

"What type of an idea?" asked Goose, looking nervously from Father Christmas to Mr. Jingelton and Mrs. Christmas and back again.

"A marvellous one!" he exclaimed. "A marvellous one that will make everybody happy, save us a lot of time, and make sure that at least something positive has come out of all this mess!"

"And what would that be?" Mr. Jingelton asked.

"Let me tell you! Gather round!"

They did as they were told, but the three of them were sure they had never seen Father Christmas look as excited as he did now.

36

FATHER CHRISTMAS WAS really pleased with his idea, and he couldn't wait to see it brought to life later that evening.

He pecked Mrs. Christmas on the cheek, and then told Goose to inform the Court of the Naughty and the Nice that he was on his way back over. Goose did as he was told, and scurried off in advance.

"Good luck, darling," Mrs. Christmas said, as Father Christmas waved behind him, as himself and Mr. Jingelton began to make their own back to the Court through the HQ.

Everybody stopped and watched him as he went as he made his way back through again — all of the Elves and Goblins were unsure as to what had happened, but they knew they wouldn't be getting any answers anytime soon.

"I hope you're all doing well today," Father Christmas said as he made his way through the business. "I think you're all doing a great job!"

A gathering of greetings floated back to him through the air. "Thank you, Sir, thank you, Sir, we're all very good, Sir, very good, Sir."

He smiled back at them, and then gave them a wave back. “Keep it up. It’s all going to be worth it.”

But the closer he got back to the Court, the smile began to fade, because he was reminded about just how much was at stake here. He may have come up with what he called a marvellous idea, one of his best ones, he had said, but if the Court found him guilty, then there was no point in hoping for anything — they’d find him guilty and then they’d rule he could no longer do the job. He’d have to leave there and then, and then what would happen to the North Pole? It was something he didn’t want to think about. He couldn’t think about it. He needed to be positive. He needed to win this court case. He had no choice but to win it.

He reached the doors of the Court, and another set of Security Goblins stepped forward and pulled them open. Everybody in the audience suddenly turned round to face him, and Father Christmas gulped. If going into the Court had been worrying the first time, going into it this second time felt even worse, especially now he had come up with his idea. He felt as though he had even more to lose now than he had done just under an hour ago before — because of his plan, depending on what the Court ruled, then it was all or nothing. There was no in-between…

Walking into the circle that still reminded him of a circus, Father Christmas and Mr. Jingelton joined Goose, who was already there and waiting for them, and stood next to their lawyer.

Once again Judge Harper walked into the room.

"Thank you for your patience, the people of the Court," she said, addressing the audience. "You may all resume your seats."

They all sat down, and she sat down along with them, getting comfortable in her seat. Father Christmas couldn't help but think she looked like some sort of a bird of prey perched up there, looking down upon them all as though she was about the eat them for her dinner. She looked sharper than ever. She was perhaps the only person that Father Christmas had found himself to be nervous about in a very, very long time. He was usually the one who was used to running the show around these parts.

"We resume here to continue the Case as discussed previously. I have already recounted that the Court took investigations upon three Departments surrounding the events of December the First and Evergreen the Elf, and the investigations failed to find a specific incident that could have caused this. However, as the Court aforementioned in our previous Court session, we have determined it to be due to negligence from the Head Team to expand their workforce to deal with the increasing demands placed upon the HQ, and therefore the Court, namely myself, would like to charge Father Christmas and his two members of his HeadQuarters Head Team for this. However, it is down to the Jury to decide. So, obviously, we now go to the Jury."

Father Christmas felt his heart begin to hammer. This was it, he realised. This was the moment of truth — everything began to flash before his eyes. Everything he had ever done, everything he had ever worked for, everything he had planned for the future of this place. It all meant so much to him. It suddenly dawned on him just how much he would miss it all if it was torn away from him; it would feel as though a huge part of his identity had been lost. This was part of who he was — it gave him focus, gave him determination, gave him a definition, and gave him a purpose. Without Christmas — well, without Christmas, Father Christmas didn't know who he was.

The Jury looked at one another, quietly confirming their verdict, and then a man with spectacles and a kind face stood up. Father Christmas, Goose, and Mr. Jingelton watched him intently.

"Mr. Hartley," Judge Harper said. "If you would, please present the Court with the verdict that the Jury have reached on this Case."

Mr. Hartley raised his hand to his mouth, and cleared his throat, and then went to talk —

— But then he was loudly interrupted.

A thud, just like last time, went off in the corner of the room, and everybody turned to see what the sudden commotion was, including Mr. Hartley, who clapped his mouth shut once again.

It was one of Judge Harper's assistant, and she had a red envelope in her hands. Father Christmas narrowed his eyes as he watched the assistant walk briskly over to Judge Harper, and then slip her the envelope quickly. What could it be?

The Jury stood there, looking around, unsure of whether they should give their verdict or not. Judge Harper opened the red envelope, and a newspaper cutting fell out of it.

"What's this?" she muttered to her assistant, but her assistant was aware that everybody was watching them.

"Just read," she said, politely but pointedly.

Judge Harper furrowed her brows, then averted her eyes to the cutting. They darted back and forth as she took the text in, and then — when she reached the end — let it fall onto her desk and looked back up at her assistant.

"This changes everything," Judge Harper said. "Everything."

The assistant nodded, then turned away and left the Court — the Court that was now left in silent suspense, waiting to hear the turn of events.

"Jury," Judge Harper said, "I am afraid I no longer need to hear a Verdict, however I am appreciative of your time."

The members of the Jury looked to one another, evidently confused, but the member who had been about to announce the Verdict sat down nonetheless. In a way, he looked a little disappointed that now he wasn't going to be able to say it — it had probably been a small, secret dream of his for many years to be able to call "Guilty!" in the middle of the Court

Judge Harper then turned to face Father Christmas, Goose, and Mr. Jingelton.

"I am well aware that you are all probably wondering what's going on," she said.

"You can say that again," Goose said.

"And I can appreciate that. But, this interruption comes as good news. Good news for you."

"In what way?" Father Christmas asked. He was confused, at a loss as to what was happening, or why this sudden change in events were suddenly taking place.

"In this envelope my assistant brought me, was a newspaper cutting. A newspaper cutting from a tabloid entitled the Northerly Herald. Does this mean anything to you, Sir?" Judge Harper asking, looking upon Father Christmas a very curious expression written across her face.

Father Christmas frowned. "Why, yes — yes, it does. The Northerly Herald is the very newspaper that has been nothing but a nuisance over this month. They're the publication that have been writing nonsensical writings about me since the very First of December."

Judge Harper nodded, placing her elbows on the surface of her desk and putting her fingertips together, as though she was deep in thought, as though pieces of a puzzle were beginning to fall into place now that she could put two and two together, and draw up a conclusion.

"Is that so?"

"That is correct," Father Christmas said back. "May I… may I ask why?" he inquired.

"This newspaper cutting from The Northerly Herald is from the issue that was published today. This very publication here, in fact, details the on-goings of this Court from this morning — more specifically, the details surrounding this very case. I made it very clear that nobody could be allowed into the Court that was from a newspaper, magazine, or any other news-source, Sir. This means that The Northerly Herald has broken the law by going against what I have ruled, but — even more specifically — means they are undercover within the North Poles HeadQuarters and reporting to the outside, which means…"

"Which means it all suddenly makes sense!" exclaimed Father Christmas, and then that was it and his brain was go, go, go, and everything — everything — was finally making sense and clicking into place and all becoming clear to him.

"News has been leaking to the public all month," Father Christmas said. "Some strange incidents have been going in this HQ this month, Judge Harper, and some of them I've learned about through actually reading the newspapers. It's almost as if—"

"It's almost as if," Judge Harper picked up, "somebody has set you up. As though somebody has snuck into the North Pole HeadQuarters, purposefully caused trouble, and then been reporting about it in The Northerly Herald, and obviously selling a lot of copies whilst they've been at it. I must admit," Judge Harper said, "as much I hate to say this, I am afraid, but I must admit it a rather clever plan — but a terrible one, and an illegal one, at that."

She slammed her hammer on the surface of her dock and then rose to her feet. "I want the Head of The Northerly Herald newspaper bringing to me — and I want them bringing to me ASAP!"

Father Christmas couldn't believe his luck.

Goose was putting everything together in his mind.

Mr. Jingelton couldn't process what he was hearing.

The audience were in shock.

The Jury in disbelief.

The poor Goblin who was sat discreetly in the audience panicking with no way of escaping now.

Things were only about to get worse, he thought to himself, because Judge Harper had barely heard half the story for now…

37

EDWINA DICKINSO WAS very pleased with herself. The latest issue had now gone to print, and she managed it — she had managed to get the story of what was going on in Court to print, and she had managed to be the only person to get the story published. Nobody else had been able to get a hold on it — which made her story an exclusive, and everybody would want to read it. Whether they supported Father Christmas or not, curiosity and sheer nosiness always gets the better of people, and so she knew it would sell — and sell very well whilst it was at it.

She sat back in her seat, and smiled. It was always after a successful story had gone to print, when she just knew in her bones they were going to do well, that she always felt her happiest, that she felt her most successful, that she felt as though she was doing a truly good job. Edwina enjoyed what she did, but she often worried that she wasn't always the best person for the job, that perhaps somebody more successful would come along, someone who was fresher and younger with a bigger spring in their step and better ideas in their mind that they would want to implement, overtaking her and leaving her left, dazzled and confused, in the dust — she was determined to not let that happen.

Just then, when she was closing her eyes, allowing herself to revel in the moment for just a minute, her door flung open, and a tall, gangly character made of long arms and stretched legs which were all flailing about in the air madly, as though a windmill had grown legs and had decided to go on the run, came falling through. The figure was so manic it took Edwina a good few seconds to even realise who it was.

"Mr. Grit!" she exclaimed. "What on Earth has gotten into you?" she asked, jumping up.

"They're on the way! They're on the way!" he half-hollered, half-panted, from being so out of breath. "They're on the way," he said, a third time, and more calmly this time.

"Who?" Edwina asked. "Who's on their way? On their way where?"

"On their way here!"

"But WHO?" Edwina shouted, beginning to lose patience.

"The Police! The Court! They're on their way here and they're on their way now. It's all over. It's all over, Edwina. We gave it a good go but we've been discovered and that's it now. Our whole plan is foiled."

"What?" she asked.

"Are you deaf?" Mr. Grit shouted back, getting mad because he was panicking. "What is their not to understand? We're going to be going to jail for such a long time." Then: "No! No, I won't allow it. It won't happen. If they think they can send me down, then they've got everything wrong. I won't go, Edwina. I won't go. I won't allow it to happen."

"It's not like you have much choice," Edwina said.

Mr. Grit whirled around. "What!" he screamed. "Is that all you have to say? Have you not got anything more to add than that trifle?" He was waving his hands in the air again at this point. "And — and — and! It's not just me who's going to be going to jail, you know. You will be too, so don't think you're clever telling me where I'm going to be going!"

"Me?" Edwina asked, pointing at herself and laughing. "No," she said, suddenly calm. "You've got that wrong. I won't be going anywhere. It's not me who's done anything wrong. I'm just the person who's been printing the stories. I didn't do the crime — so I won't be doing the time."

"Don't be so stupid," Mr. Grit argued back, exasperated. "How can you seriously say you haven't done anything wrong? You've illegally broken into a Court, you've reported a story that should have remained confidential — which is exactly how they've figured you out — and sent a bunch of Goblins into the HQ to snoop about, mess things up, and report back to you. You seriously think you've done nothing wrong?"

"I might have done some questionable things," Edwina said, casually, "but you're the one who started all this in the first place. You're the one who caused Evergreen to fall off the top of the Tree. You're the one who's tampered with his memory with the potion! You're the one who's used Crook and made him take on that blooming identity of Kane, just so you too can break into the HQ! And — and," she added, getting really angry now, "I'm not the one who broke into the Sleigh room, or messed up the List of the Naughty and the Nice. You're the one who's done all that — not me."

"You joined forces with me!" yelled Mr. Grit. "If you joined forces with me to use to your advantage, then you accept the responsibility of half of all the crimes that have been committed!"

Edwina burst out in laughter. "No, no, no, no, no," she said. "You've got all that mistaken. That's not quite how it works."

"How do you mean?" Mr. Grit asked.

"There's not even any proof that we agreed to that stuff. It's not like either of us signed a contract — we just agreed with a mere handshake. Yes, you're right," she continued, "I suppose I might have been the one who printed the stories, but so what? I did what a journalist — what a good journalist — does, and that's find out true stories and print them."

"Except that's where you're the mistaken one," Mr. Grit argued back, "because they weren't true stories."

"Everything I've reported in my newspaper is all factual; everything that I've been written about has all truly happened."

"And why has it all happened, hmm?" pressed Mr. Grit. "Why have those stories you've written about taken place, Edwina?"

Edwina shrugged her shoulders.

"Don't play a fool with me, Edwina. You know I know you more than that. You're a clever woman, Edwina — not a stupid one, so don't act like one. Those stories only happened because they were manipulated to happen. Things were put into place to make all that trouble happen. I don't know how you think you're going to get away with this."

"I do," Edwina said.

"How?" Mr. Grit asked.

"By running!" she shouted, then she ran across to her desk, grabbed her bag, and then sprinted across the room.

Mr. Grit yelled her name, and then took off after her.

"No you don't!" he called through the building, taking off after her.

By the time he was out of the office, Edwina had somehow managed to get down the stairs and was halfway down the building.

Mr. Grit didn't want to take any chances. As Edwina reached the last floor of The Northerly Herald, Mr. Grit took a run and a jump and a deep breath, and leapt over the side of the banister that ran around the top floor. Down, down, down he fell, through the middle of the building, until he landed on the floor with a heavy thud.

He hadn't landed as gracefully as he had wanted or planned for, and he twisted his ankle slightly. He cursed it, then tried to continue running after Edwina, who was ahead of him now, and she wasn't showing any signs of slowing down.

As she ran, she heard the thud and stopped momentarily to look over her shoulder, unsure of what the sound had been, when she saw Mr. Grit land funnily. He definitely didn't have the ability nor the agility of landing like a cat would. He looked up after cursing his ankle, which Edwina wasn't surprised he had hurt at all, and was — horribly but secretly — pleased about it. It might give her the chance to gain a bit of distance, give her the chance to get away from him.

She clocked him notice her, and she turned back around again, began running as fast as she could and breaking into a sprint.

"Go, go, go," she called to herself, reached the glass doors of The Northerly Herald, yanking them open, and then bursting through them, and then —

WHOOOSH!

Mr. Grit saw Edwina Inksmith race into the sky but he was only a split second behind her and he hadn't had the time to truly register what had happened to her, when he, too, burst out of the door behind her, and then —

WHOOOSH!

Into the sky he went.

The world spun and bounced around a lot, and it was only after a few dazed seconds when it all slowed down again, that Mr. Grit and Edwina were able to look around and beneath them, and realise that they had been caught.

They were both in a large net each, hanging and swinging above the ground.

"Mr. I. C. Grit and Ms. Edwina Inksmith," called up a squat Goblin from below, wearing a neat blue Police uniform and brandishing a badge in the air which glimmered silver, proving that he was a legitimate police officer of the Court of the Naughty and the Nice,

"I am pronouncing you both under arrest for a series of crimes that the two of you have committed, including but not limited to breaking and entering, fraud, and illegal mis-reporting, etc."

"You can't prove anything," Edwina said, clutching onto the strings of her net and looking down. Mr. Grit thought she looked like a mad-lady.

"We can," the Police Goblin shouted back up to the net. "Whilst we were preparing these nets, we heard everything we needed to hear from the pair of you — nice, loud, and clear, too, thank you for the shouting. I think the recording of that will be all the evidence we need, don't you?"

He smiled as he finished talking, and Edwina and Mr. Grit looked at one another through their nets, and then began cursing and shouting at one another again, blaming each other for what had happened and for being caught, accusing the other of being the one who had been too loud when they had been arguing.

The Police Goblin shook his head, asked the Police truck to back up, and asked for the crane to lower the two nets into the back of it, where their nets were secured, and then both Mr. Grit and Edwina Inksmith were sped off to jail, where they would be going for a very long time indeed.

38

THE NEWS SOON came spilling out, much to the shock of the public. None of them could believe it when they found out that a villain called Mr. Grit had been the mastermind behind it all — that he had been the one who had made Evergreen fall off the top of the tree just so he could take over Christmas and try to bring an end to it all. They had been shocked too to hear about Edwina Inksmith — she had been a journalist a lot of them had been following for many years, and many of them had respected her. They couldn't believe she would resort to sending in Goblins to act as spies to intercept the HQ, to cause trouble, to make up stories, that she could write about, and all so that she could sell more copies and make more money.

The fact that somebody could despise Christmas as much as Mr. Grit was also shocking to the people of the town. The North Pole was the place of Christmas, a place of happiness only. They felt guilty that they had ever doubted Father Christmas, and they were all sure that they were going to make it up to him. They didn't want him thinking they all thought he was bad at what he did — but Father Christmas told them all they didn't have to feel bad. He told them that under the circumstances he could understand why they had all believed what they had all believed, and that was only because they had been manipulated. This made everybody feel better, and it made Father Christmas happy to know that everybody was feeling happy again.

Crook came clean right away, and quickly told the Police Goblins and Judge Harper where the Goblins were that had been kidnapped. They were all rescued from their homes, and they were all looked after, and were told they could talk about what they had been through if it would make them feel any better, because talking always helped. They were just glad to be rescued. Crook's twin brother, Bong, realised that Bing was really Crook, who had been pretending to be Kane, and quickly reached out to his twin brother. Bing told Bong that he had made a massive mistake, and he himself told Judge Harper how he had been led into this plan because he hadn't seen any other option, and he offered his full regret at playing any part. Judge Harper had already learned that Bing had been pressured into assisting the operation by the threatening behaviour from Mr. Grit, and so she deemed that Bing only had to do a couple days of giving something back to the community over the festive period, but apart from that she was confident that his lesson had been learned and that he was ready to come back to the North Pole HeadQuarters. Father Christmas himself listened very intently to Bing, and he said that they could discuss a new job role for him to do within the HQ, so that he enjoyed his job a lot more. To this Bing was very appreciative, and decided to return to the North Pole, much to his twin brother's delight. Bong had missed Bing an awful lot over the year Bing had been gone, and Bing himself had to admit he had missed Bong too, a lot more than he had realised. He vowed to never just walk out again. He became the first person in history to have a Banishment reversed by the Court of the Naughty and the Nice, thank you to the generosity of Judge Harper.

Gordon and the other Goblins were also given the same punishment — they had to prove they all learned their lesson, and also give something back to the community over the festive period. They were all happy to do this, and Judge Harper was understanding of the fact that they had felt pressured to do what they were told from Gordon, but that Gordon wasn't to blame — because Gordon himself had only felt pressured to do what he had done thank you to Edwina Inksmith.

Father Christmas was over the moon with happiness — and over the moon quite literally, too, flying out as soon as the story had all come out once Mr. Grit and Edwina Inksmith had admitted to everything they had said during their argument after it had been played in the Court of the Naughty and the Nice for everyone to see and hear, and sent down to jail. Everybody had cheered and applauded at the verdict and its ruling, and had congratulated and apologised to Father Christmas for their recent behaviour, but he had shook them all away. They had all rushed outside as Father Christmas had announced he needed to snap to it and get back to his sleigh, which by now had finished being repaired and was spick and span and as good as new, if not better! They all formed a long stretch either side of the runway, and they watched as he and the reindeers, with Rudolph and his red nose at the front, galloped off at a run and took off into the velvety night sky, silver stars glimmering and twinkling as they watched, speeding off, across the moon, and raced off towards the rest of the world to make the world happy and perform his magic.

Most importantly, it was Evergreen himself who came out the happiest. As soon as the whole story was recounted to him, he burst out in tears because it all finally made sense. He hadn't been going mad, and he was relieved to know that there weren't any true problems with his memory. Before Edwina Inksmith and Mr. Grit were sent to jail for a very long time indeed, Mr. Grit was made to make up a remedy that could be given to Evergreen in order to be able to reverse the effects of the potion he had been slipped to tamper with his memory. As soon as he had it, it was as if all the memories were sorted back out again and put back in an order that actually made sense, much to his relief. He suddenly realised just how much he had done — he couldn't believe he had been the one to mess up the List of the Naughty and the Nice but thankfully this had been fixed right away. He felt as though this was the end of everything, and that he could move on with things now — except he didn't want to be the Star Elf anymore — as much as he had enjoyed being presented with the award, and as much as he knew it was because of what Mr. Grit had decided to do to him, Evergreen made a pact that he would stay away from Christmas trees from now on.

He wiped his eyes as he watched Father Christmas, the reindeers, and the sleigh vanish in the distance, feeling emotional. It had been a difficult month, but everything had worked out in the end. Justice had been served, the villains were behind bars, the goblins who had been involved were happy to be free again, Bing and Bong had been reunited, the townsfolk remembered just what Christmas was all about again and felt more festive than they had ever felt before. Father Christmas was more determined than ever to make sure that the boys and girls and all the grown-ups in all the lands had the best Christmas they had ever woken up to.

As he turned away from the night sky and felt the hum and the love of all the people around him, Evergreen fell deep in thought, because if they was one thing that Evergreen was sure about — more sure than he had ever been about anything else — is that it would take more than a terrible villain and money-hungry journalist to bring him down.

He was the elf that could never forget about Christmas, after all, no matter how much you tried, and that was just the way it was.

The End

More books from Josh Baldwin are coming soon!

Follow him for news on Twitter @JoshB_xx and at his website joshbaldwin.org

Printed in Great Britain
by Amazon